William Edward Armytage Axon

Folk Songs and Folk-speech of Lancashire

On the Ballads and Songs of the County Palatine

William Edward Armytage Axon

Folk Songs and Folk-speech of Lancashire
On the Ballads and Songs of the County Palatine

ISBN/EAN: 9783744784757

Printed in Europe, USA, Canada, Australia, Japan

Cover: Foto ©Andreas Hilbeck / pixelio.de

More available books at **www.hansebooks.com**

FOLK SONG

AND

FOLK-SPEECH OF LANCASHIRE

ON THE BALLADS AND SONGS OF THE COUNTY PALATINE,

WITH NOTES ON THE DIALECT IN WHICH MANY

OF THEM ARE WRITTEN,

AND AN APPENDIX ON LANCASHIRE FOLK-LORE.

BY

WILLIAM E. A. AXON, F.R.S.L.,

Author of " The Literature of the Lancashire Dialect :
A Bibliographical Essay ;" " The Black Knight of Ashton," &c.

MANCHESTER:
TUBBS AND BROOK, 11, MARKET STREET.

PREFACE.

THE following pages are an attempt to give a bird's eye view of the popular literature of the County Palatine. A paper contributed to the Saint James's Magazine has formed the groundwork of the present Essay, but the six or eight pages of that article have been extended to the size of the present publication by the desire of giving a comprehensive survey of our folk-literature.

Those who desire to extend their acquaintance further than these pages will guide them, may avail themselves of the following works :—

Gems of Thought and Flowers of Fancy. Edited by Richard Wright Procter. London, 1855.

Palatine Anthology : a Collection of Ancient Poems and Ballads relating to Lancashire and Cheshire. Edited by James Orchards Halliwell, F.R.S. London, 1850. 4to.

Palatine Garland : being a selection of Ballads and Fragments supplementary to the Palatine Anthology. London, 1850. 4to.

Ballads and Songs of Lancashire, chiefly older than the nineteenth century. Collected, compiled, and edited, with notes, by John Harland, F.S.A. London, 1850. 8vo.

Lancashire Lyrics : Modern Songs and Ballads of the County Palatine. Edited by John Harland, F.S.A. London, 1866. 8vo.

The Literature of Lancashire Dialect. A Biblographical Essay. By William E. A. Axon, F.R.S.L. London, 1870. 8vo.

For the further study of the grammatical idioms and peculiar words and phrases of the dialect, we may refer to the following works:—

Two Lectures on the Lancashire Dialect. By the Rev. W. Gaskell, M.A. London, 1854. 8vo.

On the South Lancashire Dialect, with Biographical Notices of John Collier, the author of Tim Bobbin. By Thomas Heywood, F.S.A. Printed for the Chetham Society, 1861. 4to. (Chetham Miscellanies, vol. iii.)

The South Lancashire Dialect. By J. A. Picton, F.S.A. Extracted by permission from the Transactions of the Literary and Philosophical Society of Liverpool. Liverpool, 1865. 8vo.

The Races of Lancashire, as indicated by the local names and the dialect of the county. By the Rev. John Davies. London, 1856. 8vo. Reprinted from the Transactions of the Philological Society.

To Mr. Thomas Hallam, a singularly accurate and minute observer of Phonetics; and to Mr. John Higson, of Lees, near Manchester, whose depth of antiquarian lore is only equalled by his readiness to impart it to others, I am under obligation for much assistance.

Strangeways.

FOLK SONG

AND

FOLK SPEECH OF LANCASHIRE.

TO many minds the name of Lancashire conveys only ideas of cotton. It exists in their vocabularies merely as a synonyme for a place of wondrous wealth and immense manufacturing energy,—a district where Gold reigns supreme, and where men are too eager in their pursuit of riches to pay much attention to the higher aims of life. Even now, by many people, a Manchester man is supposed to have a huge pocket, instead of the head and heart usually accorded to the sons of Adam. Even now, there are persons whose idea of the scenery of Lancashire is derived from seeing the smoky, grimy streets of Manchester, and who listen with feelings of incredulity to those who speak of her pleasant cloughs and murmuring rindles.

And yet "time-honoured Lancaster" can boast of scenery as beautiful as any in the land; and we, who have been nursed in her lap, look with pride on her fertile valleys, decked with pleasant farms, "bosomed high in tufted trees," even although in their neighbourhood may be heard the noise of the steam-engine and the whirr of the shuttle. Dear to us is the old county, with its hill-side tarns, its brown moors, green lanes, and spreading trees. Her merchant princes have ever been ready with liberal hand to encourage art and intelligence of every class, as the noble public institutions of the county amply testify; and those who think of her humbler sons as mere human calico-spinning machines, would alter their views if they visited them in their homes. There they would meet men who, toiling all day long in the factory or the machine shop, devote their leisure hours to studying the plants and flowers which deck the bosom of old mother earth. Others sedulously fill case after case with rare and beauteous entomological specimens. Some are numismatists, others dabble in antiquities; nor have the followers of James Butterworth and other self-taught mathematicians yet died out. Every village and hamlet, almost, has its library of one sort or another, and the contents of some of these storehouses of knowledge would greatly astonish the subscribers to Mr. Mudie.

> "Nor is there wanting 'mid the busy throng,
> The tuneful echoes of the poet's song."

Indeed, so numerous are the singers becoming, that they bid fair to make their quaint, strong dialect as rich in literature as the Scottish Doric of Robert Burns.

> "The poet in a golden clime was born,
>   With golden stars above ;
> Dowered with the hate of hate, the scorn of scorn,
>   The love of love ;

and endowed with quicker eye, and finer brain, and kindlier heart than ours, he can, like melancholy Jacques,

> "Find tongues in trees, books in the running brooks,
> Sermons in stones, and good in everything."

Mankind, in general, are of the same class as that Peter Bell, to whom

> "A primrose by the river's brim,
> A yellow primrose was to him,
>   And it was nothing more."

although to the poet it might give rise to "thoughts that lie too deep for tears," thoughts which he could not "half express, yet dare not all conceal."

The poet stands aloof from his fellow-men, and clad in singing robes he interprets to all who choose to hear the mysterious symbols written in the book of Nature, the tendernesses and solemnities of this visible world, the hopes, fears, and passions of the human race, even as the priest of old stood in his robes of holiness, revealing to the hosts of Israel the commands of the Lord God of Sabaoth. The poet sees with an observant eye the beauties of external nature ; to him, the brook that ripples o'er the many-coloured stones with soothing song, the trees with whose luxuriant leaves the summer winds do play, the buzzing bee that rifles from each flower its "own peculiar sweet," each rock, each stone, is unto him a book wherein he reads lessons of truth, of pity, and of love. The heart of man lies open to his view, from the sorrows and struggles of his own mind he acquires dearly bought wisdom; and these lessons he sings unto his fellow-men, pouring his very soul into the lay, and making a melody as sweet as that which wells from the breast of Israfel, "whose heartstrings are a lute, and who hath the sweetest voice of all God's creatures."

We have compared the poet's office to the solemn functions of the Hebrew priesthood; unlike the priest the poet is of no particular tribe, and one of the race of Issacher, crouching between two burdens, who has bowed his shoulders to bear, and become a servant unto tribute, is as likely to receive the poet's chrism as one of the saintly line of Levi.

The earliest relic we possess of English poetry was written by a ploughman, and since Cædmon sung the wrath of the All-father, many a son of toil has put on singing robes, and uttered strains which the world will "not willingly let die." The majority of our Lancashire singers are working men. Waugh, Bamford, Prince, Laycock, Procter, James Dawson, Jun., Ramsbottom, are all of them sons of the soil, and not mere rhymers, but men who have drunk deeply of the Heliconian spring—men who

> " On honey-dew have fed,
> And drunk the milk of paradise."

The older Lancashire ballads have, as a rule, very

little of literary excellence about them; nevertheless they are worthy of preservation, and sometimes throw a curious light upon the social history of the past. The "Bewsey Tragedy," the "Trafford and Byron Feud," are not without interest, but it is not due to the charms of poetry. Of our Jacobite relics almost the only one of merit is the "Preston Prisoners to the Ladies about Court and Town." The May songs, which Mr. Harland mentions, are not without merit, and the "Liverpool Tragedy" is a curiously barbarous version of that incident said to have occurred at Perin, in Cornwall, in September, 1617, and on which Lillo founded his tragedy of Fatal Curiosity.

The song of Lady Bessy—that is, the Princess Elizabeth, afterwards wife of Henry VII.—has an historical value. "The Tyrannical Husband" exhibits considerable humour, but our Lancashire version is a mere fragment. The subject is a favourite one with the old ballad-mongers, and various songs relating the misadventures of the goodman who would undertake the goodwife's duties are extant.

"Fair Ellen of Radcliffe" is a horrible domestic tragedy, related in the most homely style. There is but one step from the sublime to the ridiculous, and the old rhymer has unhesitatingly taken it.

In this, as in other matters, Lancashire is chiefly noticeable for what has been done within the present century. Beyond it she does not possess many lyrics of much note or beauty.

There are some exceptions to this rule, for instance

the charming old song of the Lancashire Witches, and Byrom's quaintly intricate and pleasant song of Careless Content, of which we quote a verse,—

"I am content, I do not care,
Wag as it will the world for me;
When fuss and fret was all my fare,
It got no ground as I did see;
So when away my caring went,
I counted cost, and was content."

The most interesting portions of the Lancashire anthologies, in our estimation, are those which contain the home songs of the Lancashire people, the work-a-day literature of that great hive of modern industry. The strains which, appealing to the hearts of the people, have become household words; the songs that are sung to the accompaniment of the flying shuttle, that go echoing through the noisy mill, and fill the workman's cottage with pleasant music; the melodies that may be heard alike in the streets of smoky Manchester, and in the green country fields on pleasant summer evenings.

The majority of these popular lyrics are written in the Lancashire dialect, and are occupied with the details of the sufferings and enjoyments of the daily life of the people. Side by side with this poetical literature there has grown up a prose literature of similar object and extent. With the view of illustrating fully the peculiarities of the county folk-speech, we shall take a rapid survey of its literature, illustrating the subject with extracts from both the poetical and prose works written in the dialect. With the exception of some early metrical romances, the oldest poem in the Lancashire dialect is the popular ballad of—

WARRIKEN FAIR.

Now, au yo good gentlefoak, an yo won tarry,
I'll tell yo how Gilbert Scott soud his mare Barry;
He soud his mare Barry at Warriken fair,
But when he'll be paid, he knows no, I'll swear.

So when he coom whom, an toud his woife Grace,
Hoo stud up o' th' kippo, and swat him o'er th' face,
Hoo pick'd him o' th' hillock, an he fawd wi a whack,
That he thout would welly ha brocken his back.

"O woife," quo he, "if thou'll le'mme but rise,
I'll gi' thee au' th' leet wench i'mme that lies;"
"Tho udgit," quo hoo, "but wheer does he dwell?"
"By lakin," quo he, "that au conno tell.

"I tuck him for t'be some gentlemon's son,
For he spent twopence on me when we had dun,
An' he gen me a lunchin o' denty snig poy,
And by th' hond did he shak me most lovingly."

Then Grace hoo prompted her neatly and fine,
And to Warriken went o' We'nsday betime;
An theer too hoo staid for foive market days,
Till th' mon wi' th' mare were cum t' Rondle Shay's.

An as hoo wur resting one day in hur rowm,
Hoo spoy'd th' mon a-riding th' mare into th' town,
Then bounce goos her heart, an' hoo wur so gloppen,
That out o' th' winder hoo'd loike for to loppen.

Hoo stamped an hoo stared, and down stairs hoo run ;
Wi' hur heart in hur hont, an hur wynt welly gone ;
Hur head-gear flew off, an' so did her snood ;
Hoo stamped, an' hoo stared, as if hoo'd bin woode.

To Rondle's hoo's hied, an hoo hov up the latch,
Afore th' mon had tied th' mare gradely to th' cratch !
"My good mon," quo hoo, "Gilbert greets you right merry,
And begs that you'll send him th' money for Berry."

"Oh money," quo he, "that connot I spare ;"
"Be lakin," quo hoo, "then I'll ha' th' mare."
Hoo poo'd an hoo thrumper'd him sham' to be seen,
"Thou hangman," quo hoo, "I'll poo out thy e'en.

"I'll mak thee a sompan, I'll houd thee a groat,
I'll auther ha' th' money, or poo' out thi throat ;"
So between 'em they made such a wearisom' din,
That to mak 'em at peace Rondle Shay did come in.

"Come, fye, naunty Grace, come, fye, an be dun ;
Yo'st ha th' mare, or th' money, whether yo won."
So Grace geet th' money, an whomwards hoo's gone,
But hoo keeps it hursell, and gies Gilbert Scott none.

It must be confessed that this first portrait of a
"Lancashire Witch" is not painted in very gentle
colours,—one can better admire her energy and perseverance, than her gentleness and womanly grace. As
she evidently possesses the stronger brain of the two, it
is perhaps best for poor Gilbert Scott that Naunty
Grace should constitute herself the treasurer of the
household. The authorship of this song is not known,
but "its date is fixed by the name 'Rondle Shays,'
in the fifth verse; for the name of Sir Thomas Butler's

bailiff in the reign of Edward II. (1548) was Randle Shay or Shaw."

In Richard Braithwait's Two Lancashire Lovers (1640) there is one Master Camillus, a country clown, who woos the dainty heroine in this gallant and courtly style, which we hardly recognize as the Lancashire vernacular :—

"Yaw, Iantlewoman, with the saffron snude, you shall know that I am Master Camillus, my mothers anely white boy. And she wad han you of all loves to wad me : And you shall han me for your tougher. We han store of goodly cattell : for horne, hare and leather, peepe here and peepe there, au the wide dale is but snever to them. My mother, though she bee a vixon, shee will blenke blithly on you for my cause ; and we will ga to the Dawnes, and slubber up a Sillibub : and I will look babbies in your eyes, and picke silly cornes out of your toes ; and we will han a whiskin at every rush-bearing ; a wassell cup at yule; a seed-cake at Fastens; and a lusty cheese-cake at our sheepe-wash. And will not au this done bravely Iantlewoman ?"

We find the learned and pious John Byrom was attracted to the dialect of his native county. The poems which he has written in this style are not, however, equal in merit with his *English* writings, and even these, are little read now-a-days. His charming lyric of "Careless Content" we have already quoted. Once upon a time no collection of English poems was thought complete if it did not contain his

B

pastoral of "Colin and Phebe," now almost forgotten, whilst his "Three Black Crows" lingers doubtfully in "Complete Reciters," and such like excuses for fame. As a poet his reputation may safely be founded upon that noble and mystical hymn, which at the Christmastide may be heard sweetly and solemnly rising like incense from every Lancashire valley, and from every Lancashire town. This carol alone will keep his memory green as one of the "sweet singers of the church." The only piece from his pen written entirely in the dialect is a "Lancashire Dialogue occasioned by a clergyman preaching without notes," a circumstance not very remarkable although it appears to have made a deep impression upon honest James, who is disposed to deny the title of preacher to one who reads a prepared discourse :

Sich as we han I do no meean to bleeame,
But conno' cau it fairly bi that nceame.
A book may do at whooam for larning seeake,
But in a pulpit, wheer a mon shid speeake
And look at th' congregation i' their feeace,
He canno' do't for pappers in a keease.
He ta'es fro them what he mun say, and then
Just looks as if he gan it um again.
It is i'th' church, or one could hairdly tell
But he wur conning summat to himsel :
Monny a good thing, there, I ha' hard read oo'er
But never knew what preeaching was before.

John wishing to impress his interlocutor James with the full beauty of extempore discourse, by an artful question elicits from him this reminiscence of a barrister, whose eloquence had excited his admiration :

JAMES, " Remember?" Ay and shall do while I'm whick,
Haoo bravely he fund aoot a knavish trick.
He seeav'd my faither monny a starling paoond,
And bu' for him I had no bin o'th' graoond.
That was a man worth h'yearing !—if yoar mon
Could talk like him, I shid be gloppend John.
But lukko' me, thecas lowyers are au tou't
To speak their nomminies as soon as thou't :
Haoo done yo think would judge and jury look,
If onny on 'um shid go tak a book
Aoot of his pocket, and so read away ?
They d'n soon think he hadno mich to say.
Aoor honest lowyer had my faither's deed ;
But mon, he gan it th' clark o'th' court to read ;
And then, he spooak ! And if you had bu' seen—
Whoy, th' judge himsel could ne'er keep off his cen ;
The jury gaupt agen ;—and weel they meeght,
For e'ry word 'at he had said wus reeght.

John now triumphantly remarks—

Weel, Jecams,—and if a man shid be as wairm
Abaoot his hev'n as yo abaoot yoar fairm,
Dunno' yo think he'd be as pleeast to hear
A pairson mak his reeght to howd it cleear ?
And show the de'il to be as fause a foe
As that ou'd rogue the justice wus to yo ?

This taste may suffice to show the quality of the Lancashire rhymes of the witty and wise Dr. Byrom.

A different character altogether was his contemporary John Collier. Some twenty years younger than Byrom, his life had run in a very different groove.

Born in 1709-10, at Urmston, near Flixton, of which his father was for a short time schoolmaster, his early years were passed in that "iron penury," which might be expected to harass the family of "a poor curate in Lancashire, whose stipend never amounted to thirty pounds a year." He tells us that he "lived as some other boys did, content with water porridge, buttermilk, and jannock, until he was between thirteen and fourteen years of age" (1722), when he was apprenticed to a Dutch loom weaver at Newton Moor, in Mottram, where "he met with treacle to his porridge, and sometimes a little for his buttermilk." His father had intended him for the church, and with that view probably gave him a better education than would generally fall to the lot of the "fellows of the Sisyphian Society of Dutch Loom Weavers." That his father was his tutor seems certain, we never read of him attending any school, and at the mature age of fifteen he abandoned his looms for the more congenial tasks incident to the profession of a travelling schoolmaster, "going about from one small town to another to teach reading, writing, and accounts." In 1729, he became sub-master of the free school at Milnrow, which had been built in 1724, by Mr. Richard Townley, of Rochdale, mercer, and steward of Mr. Alexander Butterworth, of Belfield Hall. Mr. Butterworth endowed it with £20 per annum, the nomination of the master remaining with the owner of Belfield Hall for the time being. Belfield Hall and the other property of Mr. Butterworth were bequeathed to his steward, whose son, Colonel Richard Townley, was the friend and patron of Tim Bobbin. In 1739, the death of Rev. Robert Pearson, the head master, lead to the appointment of Collier in his place, and with slight intermission he held the post until his decease in 1786. And now commenced Collier's education of himself, and in spite of the many disadvantages of his situation he learned to draw, model, and paint, and acquired the use of the etching needle. He was a competent Latin scholar, and is said to have had some acquaintance with Anglo-Saxon. It is to be hoped that Collier's knowledge of music (another of his accomplishments) was greater than his knowledge of art, for his pictorial efforts are execrable. A book to make an artist shudder is John Collier's "Human Passions delineated," where the coarse awkward drawings fittingly set forth a humour, gross and cruel. He was a keen observer of human nature, and a frequent visitor to village ale-houses, where he picked up subjects for his burlesque pictures, and became thoroughly familiar with the county speech. He indeed styles himself "an oppen speyker o'th' dialect," and he appears to have amused himself by collecting those words in it, which are not to be found in conventional English. As aids to its proper study he was possessed of various vocabularies, Chaucer's Canterbury Tales (a Caxton), and some other early English literature. In 1746, appeared the first edition of his "View of the Lancashire Dialect: by way of dialogue, between Tummus o' Williams's, o' Margit o'

Roaphs, and Meary o' Dick's, o' Tummy o' Peggy's. Showing in that speech the comical adventures and misfortunes of a Lancashire clown, by Tim Bobbin," a work which has had an unexampled popularity, and been constantly reprinted in all shapes and sizes from that time to the present day. The success of the pamphlet induced some roguish booksellers to print private editions, which Tim bitterly resented. To circumvent them he enlarged it, and added to it some illustrative etchings, all of them, with the exception of the frontispiece, which is a spirited likeness of the author, poor both in conception and execution. Perhaps the best test to which they can be put is to compare them with the illustrations designed by George Cruikshank for the edition of 1828, which are marvels of artistic humour and finish. The humour of Collier is of the broadest nature, he revels in coarse farcial situations, in practical joking and horseplay of the rudest description. There is a glimpse of the saturnine in his face, and in his writings we find a corresponding cynical pleasure in the sight of thoughtless torture inflicted upon the unoffending. Doubtless the picture is a true one, and pourtrays faithfully some phases of Lancashire life of the last century, but we cannot accept it as a correct general delineation. The mind sees only that which it has within it, and Collier, to judge from his life, does not appear to have been one likely to discern beauty or pathos or sublimity in the lives of the humble hinds around him, even where those qualities existed. Himself, a free living, improvident man, given to self indulgence, with no very shining moral qualities, he was not likely to recognise in others virtues of which he himself was destitute.

Collier was married on the 1st of April, 1744, to Mary Clay, a Yorkshire beauty, who had been some time in London, and coming down to Milnrow, had fascinated the heart of the witty and clever schoolmaster; though they do not appear to have been a well assorted pair, the union was a happy one, and his affection for his "crooked rib," visible in various passages of his correspondence, is one of the most genial traits in his character. As their family increased, Collier took seriously to the painting profession as a means of increasing his income, and the demand for his grotesque paintings was so great that, aided by the sale of his etchings and of his bandyhewits, as he often termed his view of the Lancashire dialect, he was able to bring up his children in comfort, and even to surround himself with some of the luxuries of life. He died at Milnrow, July 14th, 1786, and is buried at Rochdale Church.

Mr. Waugh applies Shakspere's well-known words to Tim Bobbin:

> "A merrier man,
> Within the limits of becoming mirth,
> I never spent an hour's talk withal:
> His eye begets occasion for his wit:
> For every object that the one doth catch,
> The other turns to a mirth moving jest;
> Which his fair tongue (conceit's expositor)
> Delivers in such apt and gracious words,
> That aged ears play truant to his tales."

It is pleasant to find this tribute to the saturnine genius of the old schoolmaster from his more genial successor, whose greater talent is not more remarkable than is his possession of that kindliness of feeling, and healthy moral tone, not always found in John Collier.

As an example of Tim Bobbin's style, we quote his anecdote of

THE VILLAGE WISEACRE AND THE HEDGEHOG.

"A tealier e Crummil's time wur thrunk pooing turmits in his pingot, or fund an urchon ith' hadloontrean; he glendart at't lung boh cou'd mey now't ont. He whoavt his wisket oe'rt, runs whoam, an tells his neighbours he thowt in his guts ot he'd fund a think at God never mede eawt; for it had nother heead nor tele; hont nor hough; midst nor eend! Loath t' believe this, hoave a duzz'n on em wou'd geaw t' see if they coud'n mey shift to gawm it, boh it capt um aw; for they newer o won on um ee's saigh th' like afore. Then theyd'n a keawnsil, on th' eend ont wur, ot teydn fotch a lawm, fawse owd felly; het on elder, ot coud tell oytch think; for they look'nt on im as th' Hammil-Scoance, an thowt he'r fuller o leet then a glowworm. When theyd'n towd him th' kese he stroakt his beeart; sowght; an ordert th' wheelbarrow with spon-new trindle t' be fotcht. Twur dun an the beawlt'nt him away to th' urchon in a crack. He glooart at't a good while; droyd his beeart deawn, and wawtit it o'eer weh his crutch. Wheel meh obeawt ogen o'th tother side, sed he, far it sturs an be that it shou'd be whick. Then he dons his spectacles, steeart at't agen, on sowghing sed; Breether, its summot: boh Feather Adam nother did nor cou'd kersun it. Wheel me whoam ogen." *

Robert Walker, or Tim Bobbin the Second, as he was more generally called, was in every respect of life a better man than the one who first bore that pseudonym. He was born at Carrington Barn, Audenshaw, July 27, 1728, and died at Little Moss in the same neighbourhood on the 6th of May, 1803, having overstepped the appointed three score and ten by half a decade. A staunch old reformer of the true Lancashire type he struck a hard blow for liberty in the little book by which he is now best known. He appears to have been a man of kindly disposition, respected by all his friends and neighbours. He lived a quiet life of peaceful industry, and his memory should not be allowed to die out, but should be religiously preserved among the Lancashire valleys, as that of a man who, in troubled times, when free speech was not, as now, the undisputed heritage of

---

* Did Collier pick up this anecdote during his sojourn in Yorkshire? The Rev. Wm. Gaskell, who narrates the legend in his Lecture on the Lancashire Dialect, appears to have forgotten the use which Collier had made of it.

all, spoke out freely and frankly, without fear of consequences. He lies buried in Ashton churchyard, and his tombstone bears the following inscription :—"Here resteth the body of Robert Walker, late of Little Moss, who died May 6th, 1803, in the 75th year of his age. When the corroding hand of time, and the foot of the busy passenger shall have obliterated this engraving, perhaps a memento may still remain in the integrity of heart, and the wit displayed in the little pieces published by him, which will endear his memory to genius, to liberty, and to virtue."

It was in 1796, he published "Plebeian Politics; or the Principles and Practices of certain Mole-eyed Warrites exposed, by way of Dialogue between two Lancashire Clowns, together with several fugitive pieces. By Tim Bobbin the Second. Manchester : printed by W. Cowdroy, *Gazette* office, Hunter's Lane." The object of the book is to express the disapproval felt by those of the author's way of thinking of the war with France. This is done in the form of a conversation between two friendly "Jacobins," Whistle-pig and Tim Grunt, and in the course of their "cank" they present to us a very vivid picture of the social condition of the people at that period. The humour is sometimes akin to pathos in the round unvarnished tale which is delivered of daily struggles with hunger and want, and injustice. The fun is of the healthy sort, not caused by the sight of human suffering, like that of his predecessor, but good humoured laughter at folly and self-sufficient arrogance. The tone of the

book is more healthy than that of Tim Bobbin, and is
pitched in a higher key of morality. Perhaps we may
find the cause of the difference in the several objects of
the authors. Collier's, commendable enough in itself,
was to collect in one narrative all the quaint words
and phrases which he observed among his neighbours.
Walker's chief object was certainly a political one, he
wished to throw his entire influence in the scale of
peace, nor can we conceive how he could better have
strengthened the hands of the small but active
peace party in Lancashire than by the homely argu-
ments of the two neighbours, and their simple and
truthful paintings of the distress occasioned by that
cruel war. This temporary intention of the book,
and its uninviting title, have had a disastrous effect
on the lasting reputation of Tim Bobbin the Second,
and his work, of which the early editions are now
become scarce, has not of late years been reprinted,
although it is well worthy of that honour.

Our first extract is that relating to :—

"THE SADDLEWORTH SHOUTING
TELEGRAPH."

———

" Wh. Boh I'll tell theh whot Tum, owd Dick o'
Jonny o' Noggs, e Saddlewort, had a better shift thin
o' that'n, for som time abeawt latter eend o' th' last
February, after him an th' wife an four lads had'n

liv't a whole day o'nout boh abeawt a quart o' nettle
porritch an a bit ov a krust o' breawn George : he
geet up th' mornink after, an sed to th' wife, ' I'll tell
theh what, Nan, I'm very wammo this mornink, an I
conna stond for t' weave meh bit o' th' peese eawt
beawt summot t' eat, an wee'n nowt e th' heawse ;
boh I've a kratchin kom'n int' meh yed, ot iv it
awnsers, we kon toar on till I woven my wough an
peese eawt;' 'Eigh!' says Nan, 'an whot is it?'
' Wha,' says he, ' ween send eawr Ned to Jone's o'
Robin's o' Sim's o' Will's, for a quartern o' mele ; an
tell 'im eawr kase; an t' other three lads shan gooa
with 'im, an stond abeawt hawv a quarter ov a mile,
one behind another (for theaw knows ot th' shop is
abeawt hawv a mile off,) an iv eawr Ned speeds, hee'st
set up a sheawt to eawr Will, an Tum an Dick shan
sheawt to one another, an theaw'st stond at th' fout-
yate, an theaw mey ha' th' porritch on in a krak.'

' Tum. Bith' wunds Whistle Pig, ov o' th' scheeams
ot won has hyerd on (an won has hyerd o' monny a
won) this sheds o' ! won has hyerd ov a kontrivance
ot tey had'n e France, fort carry nuse a grate way in
a little time, ot tey kod'n a telegraff : Mass ! Whistle-
pig, this shall be kode th' Saddleworth sheawtink
telegraff.'

' Wh. God a massey, Tum ! theaw's kersunt it
efeath; boh, as I're tellink theh, they sent'n th' lads
off, an they stood'n oz they'rn ordert; so Ned went
into th' shop, an sed, ' I'am kom'n fort' see iv yoah'n
le' meh hav a quartern o' mele' for wee'n had nout t'

eat sun yestur mornink, boh abeawt a quart o' nettle-porritch an a breawn George krust; an wee'n nout eth' heawse.'——'Hark the' meh, Ned,' says th' shop-keeper, 'wheear did teaw leet o' theh nettles ot t'is time o' th' year; for there's none heearabeawt.' 'Wha,' says Ned, 'I went deawn into th' Watur-heawses, an leet o' som ot back o Jim Tealier's at th' war-offis, in a warm pleck ot side o' Joe o' th' Ho Meddow: an oz I're gooink fort' tell yoah, meh fether has nout boh a wough an a peese fort' weave, an hee'l gooah down to Mossley an tak it with 'im, an ther will be oather munny or papper, an hee'l pay yoah oather to neet or i'th' mornink, an a kreawn toart th' owd ot we ow'n yoah.' 'Good lad,' sed th' shopkeeper, 'theaw tells a good tale enough, iv I do oz t' seys, theawst ha't.'—So Ned eawt o' th' shop as fast oz he kud, an seet up a sheawt to Will, an Will to Tum; and Tum to Dick; an Dick to owd Nan, at fout-yate; an beh this shift hoo geet th' porritch on oz soon oz Ned had geeten th' mele int' his poke; for owd Dick o' Johnny o' Noggs sweer ut no time should be lost, for he kud goah to no wark till hee'd summut t' eat; beh this kontrivanse theh geet'n round th' porritch dish beh won kud say trapstick, after Ned koom into th' heawse wi' th' mele.'"

Another quotation will show the state of alarm in which the powers that be were kept by the rumour of conspiracies and midnight meetings.

"Tum.—Ho! eigh, eigh; I kon tell the o' abeawt it. Theaw mun kno, ther' wur a boylink whot loyal

son o'th' gally-pott, ot went eawt won afthurnoon
amung his pashonts, on oz he'r kommink toart whom
aghen, at th' edge o' dark, he met six fellos gooink a
fotchink a loom, an a bit furr he met six or seven
mooar ot had'n bin at a kokink, an presently he o'er-
took a lad, ot had mooar mischief oth inside on him,
thin truth, an he sed, "My lad, kon teaw tell meh
whot o' yond fellos ar for ?" Eigh, sez th' lad, "Ther's
for t'be a grete jakobin meetink at Ash'n Moss kneet."
"Duz teaw sey so ?" says Mr. Pake'm. "Eigh sez th'
lad, ther'll be monyoah hundurt;" Mr. Bolus wur so
feeart ot he kewart whakerink up o'th'tit, oz ill oz
Felix did before Paul when he'r pretchink to 'im, an
he tlapt th' spurs to th' tit, an rid off neck or na
joint, an akquaintot a wizeaker sun o'th' bench; an
presently ther' koom an ordthur for eawer green
hurn't warriors, an a pasel o' skotch plod-leggs ot
wur'n quarturt i'th' teawn, (sum on em kode eawt o'
the'r beds at ten o'tlock at neet), for t' gooah a shif-
tink theese jakobins; boah whot kare ther wur tayne,
fur feear o' sumbody gooink before an akquaintink
thees jakobins whot wur komink upon 'em. So they
went'n eawt o'th' teawn, an devidnt too or three ways,
for t' meet ot a sartin plek, whear they ekspekt'nt em
for t' be, ot tey kud'n soreawn'd em, when they
koom'n to th' spot. When tey koom'n there, a sartin
Mr. Wizeaker keawart 'im deawn an peept between
an th' sky an' sed, "Husht! husht! I see 'em, ther's
monyoah skore"; presently they kod'n eawt, "Disperse
yoah rogues," boah nobudy sed nout. So it wur sed

ther wur an ordthur for t' foyor : so afthur that Mr.
Wizdom keawrt 'im deawn aghen, an peept betwcen
an th' sky, and sed these jakobins are hard, for they
ston'n yond yet, an ne'er meeon' n'em : so ther wur
an ordthur for t' advanse. But oh ! whot shall e say
neaw ? for when o' koom to o', theese jakobins proo-
fnt nothing mooar thin a pasel o' turf stakes. Boh
theaw'd a laight the sides sore for t' hah seen 'em
a komn bak aghen, for theaw'd a sworn ot sumbody
had sent a wholesale ordthur a boots amung 'em,
theydn bin up to th' knees i'th' moss doytches, so ot
the'r plod hoze wur'n nout to be seen on. An a this'n
eendot this kuiksotik ekspedeshon."

The Greenside Wakes-Song is not much more
modern than the days of Tim Bobbin. Greenside is
a small hamlet near Droylsden, and this wakes cus-
tom was imported about 1814, from Woodhouses,
" where it had been prevalent for more than the third
of a century." Two men, one of them being dressed
to represent a woman, rode in a ceremonious manner,
each of them spinning flax, and engaged in a dialogue,
which shows the progress and amicable winding up
of a domestic dispute as to their relative skill. This
song has been printed with the music in Chambers's
Book of Days, as well as in Mr. Harland's volume,
from which we now quote it :

DROYLSDEN WAKES SONG.

He

It's Dreighlsdin wakes, un wey're comin' to teawn,
To tell yo o' somethin' o' great reneawn.

Un if this owd jade ull lem'mi begin,
Aw'l show yo how hard un how fast aw con spin.
CHORUS.—So its threedywheel, threedywheel, dan, don, dill, doe.

She.

Theaw brags o' thisel, bur aw dunno think it's true,
For aw will uphowd thi, thy fawts arn't a few,
For when theaw hast done, un spun very hard,
O' this awm weel sure, thi wark is marr'd.

So its threedywheel, &c.

He.

Theaw saucy owd jade, theaws'dt best howd thi tung,
Or else awst be thumpin thi ere it be lung,
Un iv 'ot aw do, theawrt sure for to rue,
For aw con ha' monny o one as good as you.

So its threedywheel, &c.

She.

Whot is it to me whoe yo con have ?
Aw shanno be lung ere aw'm laid i' my grave ;
Un when ut aw'm deod, un have done what aw con,
Yo may foind one ot'll spin as hard as aw've done.

So its threedywheel, &c.

He.

Com, com, mi dear woife, aw'll not ha' thi rue,
Un this aw will tell yo, an aw'll tell yo true,
Neaw if yo'll forgie me for what aw have said,
Aw'll do my endavur to pleos yo instead.

So its threedywheel, &c.

She.

Aw'm glad for to yeor 'ot yo win me forgive,
Un aw will do by yo as long as aw live ;
So let us unite, an live free fro o' sin,
Un then we shall have nowt to think at but spin.

So its threedywheel, &c.

Both.

So neaw let's conclude an here eendeth our sung,
Aw hope it has pleost this numerous throng ;
Bur iv it 'os mist, yo neednt to fear,
Wey'll do eawr endevur to pleos yo next year.

     So its threedywheel, threedywheel, dan, don, dill doe.

About the end of the last century a local song entitled " Owd Ned's a rare strung chap " was very popular, far more so than it deserved, for it is destitute of literary merit. Perhaps the following song may be slightly older than the one just named. It was at one time very popular in Lancashire, and gave rise to a phrase which is still occasionally heard, "A mon o' Measter Grundy's." The meaning of the phrase may be seen from the ballad :—

" Good law, how things are altered now,
  Aw'm grown as foine as fippence ;
Bu' when aw us't to follow th' plough,
  Aw ne'er could muster threepence.
Bu' zounds, did you but see me now,
  Sit down to dine on Sundays,
Egad, you'd stare like anything
  At th' mon o' Measter Grundy's.   Ri to ral, &c.

" Aw us't to stride about i' clogs
  As thick as sides o' bacon ;
Bu' now my clogs as well as hogs
  Aw've totally forsaken ;
An' little Peg I lik't so well,
  An' walk't out upo' Sundays,
Aw've left, an now it's cookmaid Nell,
  An' th' mon o' Measter Grundy's.

C

"One day aw met my cousin Ralph;
  Says he, 'How art ta, Willie?'
'Begone,' says aw, 'thou clownish elf,
  An' dunno be so silly.'
'Why, do'st forget since constant we
  To market trudged o' Mondays?'
Says aw, 'Good lad, don't talk to me,
  Aw'm th' mon o Measter Grundy's.'

"'Egad,' said Ralph, 'who arta now?
  Aw thought no harm i' spaykin;
Aw've seen the day thou's follow'd th' plough,
  An' glad my hand were shakin';
But now, egad, thou struts about
  So very fine o' Sundays,'
Says aw, 'Thou country clod, get out,
  Aw'm th' mon o' Measter Grundy's.

"On good roast beef an' buttermilk,
  Awhoam aw lived i' clover,
An wished such feasting while aw lived,
  It never might be over;
Bu' zounds, did you but see me now
  Sit down to dine on Sunday's,
Egad, you'd stare like anything
  At th' mon o' Measter Grundy's.

"Now aw'm advanced from th' tail o' plough,
  Like many a peer o' th' nation,
Aw find it easy knowing how
  T' forget my former station;
Who knows bu' aw may strut a squire,
  Wi' powder't wig o' Sundays,
Though now content to be no more
  Than th' mon o' Measter Grundy's?"

At the commencement of the present century, a family named Wilson, who were all skilled in rhyming, gave a new impetus to this class of literature. Their songs are all marked by the same characteristics; great descriptive power and an artistic perception of the ludicrous and amusing points in every scene which they paint, combined with a rare knowledge of Lancashire nature, and a complete mastery over its dialect, have given their poems an enduring popularity among the people for whom they sang. As pictures of local life and manners they are singularly accurate and vivid, and in some respects they are still faithful pictures, notwithstanding the many changes which have taken place since they were written. The best of these songs, and the one that has been most widely popular is

JOHNNY GREEN'S WEDDIN'.

BY ALEXANDER WILSON.

Neaw lads, wheer ar yo beawn so fast?
Yo happun ha no yerd whot's past;
Aw getten wed sin aw'r here last,
    Just three week sin, come Sunday.
Aw ax'd th' owd folk, an' aw wur reet,
So Nan an' me agreed tat neight,
Ot if we could mak boath ends meet,
    We'd wed o' Easter Monday.

That morn, as prim as pewter quarts,
Aw th' wenches coom an' browt th' sweethearts,
Aw fund we're loike to ha' three carts,
    'Twur thrunk as Eccles wakes mon;

We don'd eawr tits i' ribbins too—
One red, one green, and tone wur blue,
So hey! lads, hey! away we flew,
   Loike a race for th' Ledger stakes, mon.

Reight merrily we drove, full bat,
An' eh! heaw Duke and Dobbin swat;
Owd Grizzle wur so lawm an' fat,
   Fro soide to soide hoo jow'd um;
Deawn Withy Grove at last we coom,
An' stopt at Seven Stars, by gum,
An' drunk as mich warm ale an' rum,
   As'd drown o' th' folk i' Owdham.

When th' shot were paid, an' drink wur done,
Up Fennel street, to th' church for fun,
We donc'd like morris-dancers dun,
   To th' best aw o' mea knowledge;
So th' job wur done, i' hoave a crack,
Boh eh! whot fun to get th' first smack;
So neaw, mea lads, 'fore we gun back,
   Says aw, "We'n look at th' College."

We seed a clockcase, first, good laws!
Where deoth stonds up wi' great lung claws;
His legs, an' wings, an' lantern jaws,
   They really lookt quite feorink.
There's snakes, an' watchbills, just loike poikes
Ut Hunt an' aw th' reformink toikes,
An' thee, an' me, an' Sam o' Moik's,
   Once took a blanketeerink.

Eh! lorjus days, boath far an' woide,
Theer's yards o' books at every stroide,
Fro' top to bothum eend an' soide,
   Sich plecks there's very few so;

Aw axt him if they wurnt for t' sell ;
For Nan loikes readink vastly well ;
Boh th' measter wur eawt, so he couldna tell,
   Or aw'd bowt her Robinson Crusoe.

Theer's a trumpet speyks an' makes a din,
An' a shute o' clooas made o' tin,
For folk to goo a feightink in,
   Just loike thoose chaps o' Boney's ;
An' theer's a table carv'd so queer,
Wi' os mony planks as days i' th' year,
An' crinkum-crankums here an' theer,
   Loike th' clooas press at my gronny's.

Theer's Oliver Crumill's bums and balls,
An' Frenchmen's gun's they'd tean i' squalls,
An' swords, os lunk os me, on th' walls,
   An' bows an' arrows too, mon :
Aw didna moind his fearfu words,
Nor skeletons o' men an' birds ;
Boh aw fair hate th' seet o' great lunk swords,
   Sin th' feight at Peterloo, mon.

We seed a wooden cock loikewise ;
Boh dang it, mon, these college boys,
They tell'n a pack o' starink loies,
   Os sure os teawr a sinner ;
"That cock, when it smells roast beef,'ll crow,"
Says he ; "Boh," aw said, "teaw lies, aw know,
An' aw con prove it plainly so,
   Aw've a peawnd i' mea hat for mea dinner."

Boh th' hairy mon had miss'd mea thowt,
An' th' clog fair crackt by thunner bowt,
An' th' woman noather lawnt nor nowt,
   Theaw ne'er seed loike sin t'ur born, mon.

Theer's crocodiles, an' things indeed,
Aw colours, mak, shap, size, an' breed ;
An' if aw moot tell ton hoave aw seed,
   We moot sit an' smook till morn, mon.

Then deawn Long Millgate we did steer,
To owd Moike Wilson's goods-shop theer,
To bey eawr Nan a rockink cheer,
   An' pots, an' spoons, an' ladles ;
Nan bowt a glass for lookink in,
A tin Dutch oon for cookink in ;
Aw bowt a cheer for smookink in,
   An' Nan axt th' price o' th' cradles.

Then the fiddler struck up th' honey-moon,
An off we seet for Owdham soon ;
We made owd Grizzle trot to th' tune,
   Every yard o' th' way, mon.
At neight, oych lad and bonny lass,
Laws ! they donc'd an' drunk their glass ;
So tyrt wur Nan an' I, by th' mass,
   Ot wea leigh 'till twelve next day, mon.

In 1819 appeared a " Sequel to the Lancashire dialect by Paul Bobbin." Of this work Mr. Thomas Heywood justly remarks, " The book is extraordinarily coarse, the dialogue void of pleasantry, and the incidents improbable and disgusting."

Samuel Bamford, who is still amongst us in a green and honoured old age, is not a cultivator of the folk-speech of his native shire, having only written one humourous ballad—sufficient however to make us wish he had done more :—

TIM BOBBIN'S GRAVE.

I stoode beside Tim Bobbin's grave,
'At looks o'er Ratchda teawn ;
An' th' owd lad woke within his yerth,
An' sed, "Wheer arto beawn ?"

"Aw'm gooin' into th' Packer Street,
As fur as th' ' Gowden Bell,
To taste a Daniel's Kesmus ale."
TIM.—"Aw cud like a saup mysel."

"An' by this hont o' my reet arm,
If fro' that hole theaw'll reawk,
Theawst have a saup o' th' best breawn ale
'At ever lips did seawk."

The greawnd it sturr'd beneath my feet,
An' then aw yerd a groan ;
He shook the dust fro' off his skull,
An' rowlt away the stone.

Aw browt him up a deep breawn jug,
'At a gallon did contain ;
An' he took it at one blessed draught,
An' laid him deawn again.

Mr. Elijah Ridings also has written only one song
in the dialect, although a prolific rhymer in other
lines of literature. The solitary production has been
much admired and is entitled

ALE AND PHYSIC.

Aw'r gooin by a docthur's shop,
Ut top o' Newton Yeth ;
Un theer aw gan a sudden stop,
Un began t' be feort o' deoth.

My honds shak'd loike an aspen leaf,
Aw dithert i' my shoon ;
It seemt as dark as twelve at neet,
Though it wur boh twelve at noon.

Aw thowt aw seed the gallows tree,
Wheer th' Yorn-croft thief were swung ;
Un ut owd Nick wur takkin me,
Un theer he'd ha' me hung.

Aw grop'd my way to th' docthur's heawse,
Un then aw tumblet deawn ;
Th' floor it gan me such a seawse,
Aw welly brock my creawn.

Neaw what wur th' docthur thinking on,
Fort' bring me to mysel,
Un save a sick and deein mon,
So feort o' deoth an' hell ?

He used no lance, he used no drug,
Ut strengthens or ut soothes ;
Boh he browt some strong ale in a jug,
Ut ud come fro' Willey Booth's.

He put it in my whackerin hont,
Ut wur so pale an' thin ;
Aw swoipt it o' off at a woint,
Un aw never ail't nowt sin.

In 1851 appeared " O ful tru un pertikler okeawnt o bwoth wat aw seed un wat aw yerd we gooin too th' greyt Eggshibishun e Lundun, be o Felley fro Rachde"; it immediately took firm hold of the popular taste, and notwithstanding the ephemeral character of its subject is still one of the most

popular works in the dialect, and deservedly so.
Written in the genuine folk-speech of the Rochdale
district, its delineation of the shrewd yet ignorant
"felley," his amusing want of acquaintance with
everything five miles off Smobridge, his disregard of
proportion in his estimation and comparison of things
with which he is acquainted with those of which he
is ignorant, his genial good humour, and his demon-
strative loyalty, is an amusingly faithful picture. You
feel, however, in holding the Rachde felly by the
hand, that you are not dealing with one of Tim
Bobbin's soulless boors, but a man, touched with the
spirit of the times, and in spite of limited education,
and its consequent prejudices, one of those whose
strong hands and stronger brains have built up the
prosperity of Lancashire. We select as a specimen
the hero's account of his

VISIT TO MADAME TUSSAUDS.

Fro theere aw went ramblin obeawt till aw koome
to wat they koed Madum Tussawds, un aw went op
sum stayres, un wen aw'd pade me shillin, hin aw
went, un eh! wat a seet, fur shure — kings un
quenes be wholsale, un they fare glittert ogen. We
bein raythur tyert, aw seete mesel deawn oppo o shet
oeronent o rook o foine figgers, aside uv o owd gray-
yedded chap we o leet culurt quot on, us wor stayrin
at um loike o gud un. Thynks aw to mesel, th' owd
felley mun nevur o bin e sich o spot us this afore. E

luket so gloppent. Aw sed too im, This us o grand konsarn, mestur, iv yo plez, but E stayrt oway un nevur sed naut. Onuther mon us wor nesht to me uth tuther soide sed u must speke op, me man, the old gentulmun's o littul def. Aw sed, O is E ; but aw'l may im yer, yo's see, un aw koed eawt raythur leawd, dunnut yo thynk us this o grand konsarn : but E stayrt oway un seet theere us quoite us o meawse. Just then, aw seed tuthre foke laffin, un restin ther cen obeawt weere aw wor, un a mon tutcht me shilder un sed,—The old man's waxwurk. Sur, aw sed, nevur, fur shure ! Aw gan im a gradely stayre ith faze un aw'l be sunken iv E wornt o wax chap saime us tuther, but aut moore natteruble cuddent be dun, to maw thynkin. Whoo dun yo think it wor ? Waw it wur owd Billy Kobbitt, fur aw noed im we wonst yerin im lektur e Rachde. It wor ith Unitay-rian Chappil, un aw rekillekt verri wele us his kan-duls wantud snuffin, un o chap koed eawt ith gallure us they'rn o pare o snuffers oside on im, un Billy geet howd on um, un made us laff we sayin Aw gues o political parsun mun snuf his own kanduls. E wor o funny owd dog, wor Billy, wen E'd a moind. Sum uth figgers wor unkommun natterul, moore pertiklur thoose as turnt ther yeds reawnd, un heaw that wur dun aw connut gaum fur th' loike on me. Wen aw geet tuth fur end, o chap ax'd me iv aw'd goo hinto th' chaimbur o orrors. Aw sed wat han yo e thut orrobul chaimbur us yo koen it ? Wy E sed, o num-ber ov the biggest skoundrils that evur liv'd. Nay,

aw sed, yo'r mistaen theere, mon, fur ther's won rap-
skallion us yo shudden av in afore th' reawm ul be
gradely fit op e that loine, o biggur thefe, to maw
thynkin, nur ony us yo han theere. Whoo's that? E
sed. Waw, aw sed, o villun ov a powsedurt ov o
thefe, us rogued me eawt ov o suverin tuther day,
heaw sumevvur, aw sed, aw'l av o bit ov o pepe at um,
un aw wor gooin in, but E koed eawt, Ther's sixpunze to pay. Noane fur me, aw sed, awd o gin o
shillin rathur nur o sin that thefe us aw towd yo on,
un aw'm noane sich a foo us to gie yo sixpunze fur to
see hauve o duzzen sich loike, un we that aw turnt
mesel reawnd ogen, un wen aw'd luke't ut th' whacks-
wurk kraturs whol aw wor tyret, aw went streyt
whoame to Mestur Pike's.

The late John Bolton Rogerson, whose fame was
achieved as a lyrist, and whose charming song of
"Nothing More" will alone suffice to perpetuate
his name for long years has written one humourous
ballad in the vernacular dialect, entitled, "Th'
Ballies."

So far in our rapid survey we have seen that for more
than a hundred years the dialect has been used by
many writers known and unknown, as a suitable
vehicle for humourous narrative seldom of a very
refined character, seldom having any higher object
than to excite a laugh at the misfortunes of some
"clown." Rarely do we find any attempt to pene-
trate beyond the veil, or show us what there is of
truth, endurance, and love within the sanctuary.

Although he has had many predecessors in the use of the dialect, Mr. Waugh was the first who painted at full length, with all its lights and shades, the portrait of a Lancashire lad. He thus opened a vein of considerable richness, and although many have followed in his footsteps none have surpassed him. The pathos and simplicity of his now famous lyric "Come Whoam to thi Childher an Me," at once gave him the place as the laureate of Lancashire; and a succession of charming songs, some of which, in beauty, far excel that maiden effort bear witness to his dramatic power, and his ability to link together beauty of thought and language "in lengthened sweetness, long drawn out." Mr. Waugh was born at Rochdale in 1819, and is a self-educated man. In his youth and early manhood he was engaged as a journeyman printer. During the existence of the National School Association, he was one of its secretaries, and since then has chiefly devoted himself to literature. His philosophy is of the genial order, he is no lachrymose sage running hither and thither, and crying woe, woe, but one loving the sunny side of things, blessed with a keen enjoyment of life, a vivid perception of the beauty of nature, and deriving from it compensation for the crosses of life. The dignity and nobility of labour, the sacredness of duty, the claims of home and family, of brotherhood and humanity are the chief doctrines in his creed.

It is somewhat difficult to quote from Mr. Waugh; his songs are household words throughout the county.

As a specimen of careful Flemish painting what can
be finer than " Eawr Folk," or more spirited than its
enthusiastic finale?   The rural sweetness of the
" Sweetheart Gate," and the tendor pathos of
" Willie's Grave," show Mr. Waugh's mastery over
the varied emotions of the human heart and prove his
claim to a place among the priests of Poesy.

As a specimen of his poetic writing we select

CHIRRUP.

Young Chirrup wur a mettled cowt :
  His heart an' limbs wur true ;
At foot race, or at wrostlin'-beawt,
  Or aught he buckled to ;
At wark or play, reet gallantly
  He laid into his game :
An' he're very fond o' singin'-brids—
  That's heaw he geet his name.

He're straight as ony pickin'-rod,
  An' limber as a snig ;
An' th' heartist cock o' th' village clod,
  At every country rig :
His shinin' een wur clear an' blue ;
  His face wur frank an' bowd ;
An' th' yure abeawt his monly broo
  Wur crispt i' curls o' gowd.

Young Chirrup donned his clinker't shoon,
  An' startin' off to th' fair,
He swore by th' leet o' th' harvest moon,
  He'd have a marlock there ;
He poo'd a sprig fro th' hawthorn-tree,
  That blossomed by the way :—
" Iv ony mon says wrang to me,
  Aw'll tan his hide to-day !"

Full sorely mony a lass would sigh,
   That chanced to wander near,
An' peep into his cen to spy
   Iv luv wur lurkin' theer ;
So fair an' free he stept o'th' green,
   An' trollin' eawt a song,
We leetsome heart, an' twinklin' een,
   Went chirrupin' along.

Young Chirrup woo'd a village maid,—
   An' hoo wur th' flower ov o',—
Wi' kisses kind, i'th' woodlan' shade,
   An' whispers soft an' low ;
I' Matty's ear twur th' sweetest chime
   That ever mortal sung ;
An' Matty's heart beat pleasant time
   To th' music ov his tung.

Oh, th' kindest mates, this world within,
   Mun sometimes meet wi' pain ;
But, iv this pair could life begin,
   They'd buckle to again ;
For, though he're hearty, blunt, an' tough,
   An' Matty sweet and mild,
For three-score year, through smooth an' rough,
   Hoo led him like a child.

As an example of Mr. Waugh's skill as a prose humourist, we quote his account of

BODLE'S ADVENTURE AS A SWEEP.

"Bodle an' Owd Ned had bin upo' th' fuddle a day or two ; an' one mornin' they'd just getten a yure o'

th' owd dog into 'em, an' sit deawn afore th' kitchen
fire, as quiet, to look at, as two pot dolls. But they
did'nt feel so noather, for they'd some ov a sore yed
a piece that mornin', th' owd lads had. Well, theer
they sit, in a sort ov a slow boil, turnin' things o'er
an' gruntin', an' tryin' to spit cawt neaw an' then;
when, o' at once, Bodle, began o' lookin' yearn'stfully
at th' fire hole, an' he said, 'Aw'll tell tho what,
Ned; aw've a good mind to go up th' chimbley.'
Well, yo know'n, owd Neddy likes a spree as weel as
ony mon livin'; an' he's noan tickle what mak o'
one it is, noather; so when he yerd that, he jumped
up an' said—'Eh, do, owd lad! Go up! Up wi'
tho! Thae'rt just i' reet fettle for a job o' that mak
this mornin'!" Bodle stood a minute scrattin' his
yed, an' lookin' at th' chimbley; an' then he began o'
doublin' his laps up, an' he said,—'Well, but, neaw;
doesto rayley think 'at aw should go up, owd crater?'
'Go up? Ay! what else!' said Neddy, 'Up wi'
tho, mon! Soot's a good thing for th' bally-warche!
Beside it'll be a bit ov an cawt for tho! It's as good
as gooin' to Blackpool! Aw'd ha' gone up mysel' iv
aw'd had my Sunday clooas on. Go up! Aw'll gi'
tho a quart ov ale when tho comes deawn again!"
'Wilto, for sure?' said Bodle, prickin' his ears. 'Is
it a bargain? Come, fair doo's amoon mates!' 'Iv
aw live, an' thae lives, Bodle,' said owd Neddy,
'theawst have a quart as soon as tho comes down
again, iv ever theaw does come deawn again! Here's
my hont, owd lad!' 'Done,' said Bodle, ' an ' neaw

for summit fresh,' as Adam o' Rappers said when he roll't off th' kitchen slate into th' midden-hole. Eh, Summit Tunnel's a foo to this! But aw'll go up iv it's as lung as a steeple.' So th' owd lad made no moor bawks abeawt it but set tone foot upo th' top bar, an' crope reet up into th' smudge-hole. Just as he're rommin hissel' in at th' bothom, th' owd woman coom in to see what they had'n agate; an' when Bodle yerd her speyk, he co'd out—'Hey, Ned; houd her back a bit or else hoo'll poo mo deawn again.' Th' owd woman stare't awhile afore hoo could make it eawt, whatever it wur that wur creepin' up th' chimbley o' that shap; an hoo said, 'What mak o' lumber han yo afoot neaw? Yo're a rook o' th' big'st foo's at ever trode a floor! Yo'n some devilment agate i' th' chimbley aw declare. It's that drunken waistrel ov a Bodle, aw believe! Aw know him bi his clogs. Th' tone on 'em's brawsen. Eh thae greyt gawmless foo! Wheer arto for up theer! Thae'll be smoor't, mon!' Hoo would ha darted forrud an' gettin' hold on him, but owd Ned kept stoppin' her, an' sayin', 'Let him a-be, mon! It's nobbut a bit ov a spree. He's gone up a bit ov an arran' for me. He'll be back directly; wi' a new suit o' black on.' Then he looked o'er his shoolder, and sheawted, 'Bodle, get forrud wi' tho! Thae met ha' bin deawn again by neaw!' An' then as soon as he thowt th' owd lad wur meeterly weel up th' flue, he leet her off; but hoo wur too lat to get howd on him. Hoo could just reytch to hit him o' th' legs wi' th' poker. When he felt hur hittin' him, he sheawted deawn th' chimbley, 'Who's that 'at's hittin mo?' 'Whau,' said hoo, 'it's me, thae greyt leather-yed. Come deawn wi' tho! What arto doin' i' th' chimbley?' 'Aw'm gooin' up for ale,' said Bodle. 'Ale!' said hoo, 'there's no ale up theer, thae brawsen foo! Eh, aw wish yo're Mally wur here!' 'Aw wish hoo wur here istid o' me,' said Bodle. 'Come down wi' tho, this minit, thae greyt drunken hal,' said th' owd woman; 'or aw'll set tho a fire,—that aw will!' 'Aw cannot come back yet, aw tell yo,' said Bodle. 'There's ale at th' end o' this job, or else aw'd never ha come'n as fur up as aw ha done. But aw'll not be long, yo may depend; for its noan a nice place, this is'nt. Eh, there is some ov a smudge! An' it gwos wur as aw go fur! By guy, aw can see noan—nor talk noather. Ger off wi' yo; an' let mo get it o'er, afore aw'm chauk't!' An' then he crope furrud.

"When owd Neddy had watched Bodle draw his legs out o' sect, he set agate o' hommerin' th' chimbley-wole wi' his hont, an' sheawtin', 'Go on, Bodle, owd lad! go on, owd mon! Thae'rt a reet un i' tha loses! Thae'st have a quart o' th' best ale i' this hole, i' tho lives to come deawn again; an' i' tho dees through it, owd brid, aw'll be fourpence or fippence toward thi berrin'.' An' then he sheawted up an' deawn th' heawse, 'Hey! dun yo yer, lads! Owd Bodle's gwon up th' chimbley! Aw never sprad my e'en upo' th' marrow trick to this!' Well, th' whol heawse wur up in a snift, an rare gam they had'n.

D

Owd Ned kept gooin to th' eawtside to see iv Bodle had getten his yed eawt o' th' top, an' then runnin' in again, an bawlin' up th' flue, 'Bodle, heaw arto gettin' on? Go through wi't, owd cock! Dunnot be lick't wi' a chimbley!' But just as he wur starin' up an' talkin', Bodle lost his howd, somewheer abeawt th' top, an' he coom shutterin' deawn; an o' th' soot i'th' chimbley wi' him. Then he let wi' his hinder end thump o' th' top-bar, an' roll't deawn upo' th' har'stone, like a greyt pokeful o' sleck. Eh, what a blash-boggart he looked! Th' owd lad did'nt know wheer he wur for awhile, so he lee roll't up o' th' floor, amung a cleawd o' soot; an owd Neddy kept laughin' an' wipein' his e'en, and sayin', 'Tay thi wynt a bit, Bodle! Thae'rt safe londed, iv it be hard leetin'! It's a good job thae leet o'th soft end on tho, too, owd lad. But, when aw come to think, aw dunnot know which is th' softest end o' thee. But thae'rt a good un; bith mon arto! Tay thi wynt, owd brid! Thae'st have a quart, owd lad, as soon as ever aw con see my gate to th' bar through this smudge 'at thae's brought wi' tho! Aw never had my chimbley swept as chep i' my life, never!'"

The success of the Ratchda Felley and of Waugh's Lyrics probably lead the late John Scholes to turn his attention to the dialect. As "Sam Sondnokkur" he relates his experiences on a visit to "Manchestur Mekaniks Hinstitushun Sho"; under the disguise of "Tim Gamwattle" he narrates a "Jawnt i' Ab-o'-Dicks oth' Doldrums Waggin wi' a whull waggin full

o' foak a seeint Quene," and in other disguises re-
counts homely stories of the country side, full of
hearty, healthy laughter, and with here and there an
indication of higher power than he lived fully to express.   One of the most perfect lyrics in the Lancashire
dialect, if not, indeed, the best of its love poems, is his

LANCASHIRE WITCH.

" An owd maid aw shall be, for aw'm eighteen to-morn,
   An aw myen to keep sengle an' free ;
But the dule's i' th' lads, for a plague thi were born,
   An' thi never can let one a-be, a-be,
   They never can let one a-be.

Folk seyn aw'm to' pratty to dee an owd maid,
   An' at love sits an' laughs i' my ee ;
By leddy aw'm capt at folk wantin' to wed,
   Thi mey o' tarry sengle for me, for me,
   Thi mey o' tarry sengle for me.

There's Robin a' mill—he's so fond of his brass,—
   Thinks to bargain like shoddy for me ;
He may see a foo's face if he looks in his glass,
   An' aw'd thank him to let me a-be, a-be,
   Aw'd thank him to let me a-be.

Coom a chap t'other day o' i hallidi trim,
   An' he swoor he'd go dreawn him for me ;
Hie thi whoam first and doff thi aw sed bonny Jim,
   Or the'll spuyl a good shute, does ta see, does ta see,
   Thae'll spuyl a good shute, does ta see.

Cousin Dick says aw've heawses, an' land, an' some gowd,
   An' he's planned it so weel, done yo see ;
When we're wed he'll ha' th' heawses new fettled an' sound,
   But aw think he may let um a-be, a-be,
   Sly Dicky may let um a-be.

Ned's just volunteered into th' roifles recruits,
   An' a dashing young sodiur is he,
If his gun's like his een it'll kill where it shoots,
   But aw'll mind as they dunnot shoot me, shoot me,
   Aw'll mind as they dunnot shoot me.

He sidles i' th' lone, an' he frimbles at th' yate,
   An' he cooms as he coom no for me ;
He spers for ar John, bo' says nought abeawt Kate,
   An just gies a glent wi' his ee, his ee,
   An' just gies a glent wi' his ee.

He's tall, en' he's straight, an' his curls are like gowd,
   An' there's summat so sweet in his ee,
At aw think i' my heart, if he'd nobbut be bowt,
   He needna quite let me a-be, a-be,
   He needna quite let me a-be.

Mr. Benjamin Brierley is best known by his skill as a novelist, but he has, nevertheless, written some charming lyrics, the prettiest of them being the quaint song of the

WEAVER OF WELLBROOK.

Ye gentlemen o' with yor heawnds an' yor parks—
   Yo may gamble an' sport till yo dee ;
Bo a quiet heawse nook, a good wife, an' a book,
   Is mooar to the likins o' me-e.

Wi' mi pickers and pins,
An' mi wellers to th' shins,
Mi linderins, shuttle, and yeald-hook,
Mi treddles an' sticks,
Mi weights, ropes, an' bricks,
What a life! said the Wayver of Wellbrook.

Aw care no' for titles, nor heawses, nor lond,
Owd Jone's a name fittin for me ;
An' gie mi a thatch wi' a wooden dur-latch,
An' six feet o' greawnd when aw dee.   Wi' mi, &c.

Some folke liken't stuff their owd wallets wi' mayte,
Till they're as reawnt an' as brawsen as frogs ;
Bo for me aw'm content when aw've paid down mi rent,
Wi' enoof t' keep me up i' mi clogs-ogs.   Wi mi, &c.

An' then some are too idle to use ther own feet,
An' mun keawr an' stroddle i' th' lone ;
Bo when aw'm wheelt or carried, it'll be to get berried,
An' then dicky-up wi' owd Jone-one.   Wi' mi, &c.

Yo may turn up yor noses at me an' th' owd dame,
An thrutch us like dogs agen th' wo :
Bo as lung 's aw con nayger, aw'll ne'er be a beggar,
So aw care no a cuss for yo o-o'.   Wi' mi, &c.

Then, Margit, turn round that hum-a-drum wheel,
An' mi shuttle shall fly like a brid ;
An' when aw no lunger con use bont or finger,
They'm say,—while aw could do aw did-id.   Wi' mi, &c.

Mr. Brierley was born at Failsworth in 1825, and was
fully thirty years of age when he commenced author.
The account of his visit to Daisy Nook published un-

der the title of " A Day Out," at once showed that a
new and talented painter of Lancashire life had arisen
to share the fame of Collier and Waugh. The favour-
able impression made by this first effort has been
greatly increased by his subsequent writings, in which
he has shown not only skill in painting the daily life
of Lancashire, the loves, joys, and sorrows of the
people among whom he dwells, but a dramatic power
and freshness by no means common. But whilst the
fable of his fictions are with few exceptions ingenious
and artistic, it is unquestionably to the rare combination of humour and pathos in his characters that his
wide popularity is owing. Like Edwin Waugh's
famous fiddler he is alternately gleeful and tender :—

> An' sometimes, th' wayter in his e'en,
> 'At fun has teyched to flow,
> Can hardly roll away, afore
> It's wash'd wi' drops o woe.

The same hand that has drawn scenes as broad in
humour as any of Collier's, fun as unrestrained as a
Dutch Kermasse, has also painted that solemn scene of
Shadow's Deathbed. "Humour quaint and old-
world like," says a modern critic, " yet genial as the
newest day in summer—at times subdued and calm
as the smile on the face of a sleeping child, or gushing
forth joyously—yet ever humour ; pathos touching and
tender as the face of your dear dead girl, and leaving a
sadness in your heart, and tears in your eyes ; and wit,
bright and cutting as a Damascus blade, and bending
like one,—are thrown together in the same pages with

a magical power ; and the smile, the hearty laugh, the
quiet tear are created by reading almost any one of
Mr. Brierley's stories. The creation of such real lasting feelings is the most blessed privilege of true
genius ; it is true art, and not acquired by studying
certain cold dry rules—but the art inborn, and therefore god-given, and part of the soul. It may seem a
simple thing to make the human heart thrill with joy
or throb with pain ; but in the sense we speak of,
genius, and genius alone, can play upon the wondrous
harp, evoking wild sad laments, or glorious gushes of
thankful praise. Benjamin Brierley can do this, and
the laughter he creates is as healthy as the tears you
cannot keep back when he introduces you to such
men as ' Hobson ' and ' Shadow.' "

Perhaps after Waugh, no Lancashire songwriter
has attained such popularity as Mr. Samuel Laycock,
whose separate poems (originally published on fly-
sheets) sold to the extent of forty-thousand copies
before they were collected into permanent form as a
book, and although his writings are somewhat unequal
there can be no doubt that he amply merits the ap-
plause which he has received.

The native humour and subdued pathos of "Welcome
Bonny Brid " have made it a universal favourite, but
the finest poem he has yet produced is "Bowton's
Yard," which describes in homely rhymes the fortunes
and characters of each denizen of the now famous
yard. What a beautiful picture is that of the aged
shoemaker,

At number nine th' owd cobbler lives, th' owd chap 'at mends
   mi shoon,
He's gettin' very weak an' done, aw think he'll leave us soon ;
He reads his Bible every day, an' sings just like a lark,
He says he's practising for heaven, he's welly done his wark.

" Th' Coortin' Neet," is a faithful picture of a rus-
tic wooing, and " The Village Pedlar " is a vividly
sketched portrait of one of those characters who are
fast disappearing before the march of improvement.
As a fair specimen of Mr. Laycock's powers we quote
the following poem :—

THEE AN' ME.

Tha'rt livin at thi country seat,
   Among o' th' gents and nobs :
Tha's sarvant girls to cook thi meat,
   An do thi o thi jobs.
Awm lodgin here wi' Bridget Yates,
   At th' hut near th' ceaw-lone well ;
Aw mend mi stockins, pill th' potates,
   An wesh mi shurts mysel.

Tha wears a finer cooat nor me,
   Thi purse is better lined ;
An fortin's lavished more o' thee
   Nor th' rest o' human kind.
Life storms that rage around this yed,
   An pelt so hard at me,
Till mony a time aw've wished awrn dyed
   But seldom trouble thee.

Tha'rt rich i' o this world can give,
   Tha's silver an tha's gowd ;
But me—aw find it hard to live,
   Aw'm poor, an' gettin owd:
These fields and lones aw'm ramblin through—
   They o belong to thee ;
Aw've ony just a yard or two,
   To ceawer in when aw dee.

When tha rides eawt, th' folks o areawnd
   Stond gapin up at thee,
Becose tha'rt worth ten theawsand peawnd,
   But scarcely notice me.
Aw trudge abeawt fro spot to spot,
   An' nob'dy seems to care ;
They never seek my humble cot,
   To ax me heaw aw fare.

If tha should dee, there's lots o' folk
   Would fret an cry, no deawt ;
When aw shut up they'll only joke,
   An say, " He's just gone eawt,—
Well, never heed him, let him go,
   An find another port ;
We're never to a chap or two,
   We'n plenty moor o' th' sort."

Tha'll have a stone placed o'er thy grave
   To shew thi name an age ;
An o tha's done at's good an brave,
   Be seen o' history's page.
When aw get tumbled into th' greawnd
   There'll ne'er be nowt to show
Who's restin neath that grassy meawnd,—
   An nob'dy 'll want to know.

But deawn i' th' grave, what spoils o th' sport,
   No ray o' leet can shine,—
An th' worms below can hardly sort
   Thy pampered clay fro' mine.
So when this world for th' next tha swaps,
   Tak wi' thi under th' stone
Thi cooat ov arms, an bits o' traps,
   Or else tha'll ne'er be known.

But up above there's One 'at sees
   Through th' heart o' every mon ;
An he'll just find thee as tha dees,
   So dee as weel as t' con :
An aw'll do the same, owd friend, an then,
   Wi' o eawr fauts forgiven,
P'raps thee an me may meet again,
   An booath shake honds i' heaven.

Mr. Bealey is another most successful delineator of Lancashire character. The most beautiful of his efforts is probably his portrait of "Eawr Bessy," golden-haired child, the light of the household, who seems to have had glimpses of the asphodel valleys beyond the dark river, and who longs for the land of light and love. "Whom the Gods love die young," and so this fair and fragile flower of the flock is called away,

Aw thowt hoo're gooin', an' aw ax'd
   If hoo ud like to dee,
An' live wi' th' angels ? but hoo said,
   " Aw'd rayther stay wi' thee."

But then hoo seemed to look abeawt,
   Then fixed her little e'en ;
An sich a look coom o'er her face
   As if hoo'd summat seen.

Then stretchin eawt her little arms,
　An' lookin' up aboon,
Her e'en as breet as stars, hoo said,
　" Aw'm comin'—comin'—soon."

An' with a smile upon her face,
　Ut seemed like break o' day,
Hoo went just like a mornin' star,
　Ut dayleet melts away.

The description of " Eawr Bessy " and the mother's anguish at the death of her darling, are painted with great truth and homely pathos. In another mood altogether is " My Johnny," a simple picture of honest love, showing how Dan Cupid rules his subjects in South Lancashire. As we have only to speak here of the folk songs of Lancashire, we must omit all the more general writings of the authors we have named. For this reason we do not stay to examine Mr. Bealey's general poetry, but content ourselves with another song of his which has attained a deserved popularity, and which breathes a wise tolerance and childlike confidence in the goodness of the Father.

MY PIECE IS O' BUT WOVEN EAWT.

My piece is o' but woven eawt,
　My wark is welly done;
Aw've treddled at it day by day,
　Sin th' time ut aw begun.
Aw've sat i'th loom-heawse long enoof,
　An' made th' owd shuttle fly,
An' neaw aw'm fain to stop it off,
　An' lay my weyvin' by.

Aw dunnot know heaw th' piece is done,
　Aw'm fear'd it's marr'd enoof,
But th' warp wern't made o' th' best o' yarn,
　An' th' weft wur nobbut rough.
Aw've been some bother'd neaw and then
　Wi' knots an' breakin's too ;
They'n hamper'd me so mich at times,
　Aw've scarce known what to do.

But th' Mester's just, and weel He knows,
　Ut th' yarn wur noan so good;
He winna bate me when He sees
　Aw've done as weel 's aw could.
Aw'se get my wage, aw'm sure o' that,
　He'll gie me o' ut's due,
An' maybe, in His t'other place,
　Some better wark to do.

But then, aw reckon, 'tisn't th' stuff
　We'n gatten t' put i' th' loom,
But what we mak on't, good or bad.
　Ut th' credit on't 'll come.
Some wark i' silk, an' other some
　Ha' cotton i' their gear ;
But silk or cotton matters nowt,
　If nobbut th' skill be theer.

But now it's nee to th' eend o' th' week,
　An' close to th' reckonin' day :
Aw'll tak my "piece" upo' my back,
　An' yer what th' Mester 'll say ;
An' if aw nobbut yer His voice
　Pronounce my wark weel done,
Aw'll straight forget o' th' trouble past,
　In th' pleasure ut's begun.

The limits of an essay of this nature prevent us

from doing justice to all who have written in the dialect, we can only give a brief appreciation of the works of Joseph Ramsbottom, J. T. Staton, Thomas Brierley, Joseph Charlesworth, John Higson, George Richardson, who have all attained some popularity and success in this style of writing. Nor can we stay to particularize the talented sketches of Miss M. R. Lahee. We recognize at once the graphic portraiture of honest "Owd Neddy Fitton," and sympathise with the struggles of "Jomes Wrigley." Mr. Mellor, better known as "Uncle Owdam," is another of our Lancashire minstrels, and we venture to quote a little lyric of his entitled

LOVE THOWTS.

Oych morn when th' pattin' ov his clogs,
   Maks music close to th' cottage winder,
Aw peep through th' blind, he looks an' smiles,
   My face bruns like a red-whot cinder.
That look an' smile whol day-leet lasts,
   Are coals 'at keep my heart-foyr brunnin';
An' sometimes too such thowts 'll come,
   'At set my een agate a-runnin.

Oych neet when passin' by again,
   His face reet full o' looks so winnin',
He'll stop an' stond at th' cottage dur,
   While mother an' mysel sit spinnin'.
An' then he'll say,—so ticin' too,
   While th' roses to my cheeks are rushin',
"Come, Mary, lass! will t'have a walk?"
   Aw wonder who could help fro blushin'!

Eh ! heaw aw lung to link wi' him,
  Down th' shady lone when th' brids are singin',
Eh ! heaw aw love to yer his voice,
  So nobly an' so sweetly ringin'.
An' when he puts his face to mine,
  An' starts a smilin', then a kissin',
Eh ! heaw mi heart jumps to my meawth—
  Aw feel—aw don't know heaw—God bless him !

He's never axed mi t'wed him yet ;
  Bur well aw know he'll never lave mi ;
Nowe ! Billy is too good a lad,
  His love's too true for t'e'er desave mi.
Aw'll bide mi time,—its till he's sav't
  A bit o' brass,—he mun be waitin' ;
Hush ! that's his fuut—aye, aye, it's it !
  Eh ! heaw it sets mi heart a batein' !

It would be an easy and a pleasant task to extend
these observations on this part of our subject, by re-
ferring to the works of the writers we have named, and
others of the same class, but we hope that enough has
already been said to show how rich and varied in interest is the literature of the Lancashire folk-speech.

In the preceding extracts which form an epitome of
the history of the dialect, we have scrupulously ad-
hered to each author's orthography. Owing to the
confused and arbitrary system which Englishmen are
content to dignify by the name of spelling, this
orthography seldom conveys any idea of the pronunciation to one not already familiar with it. To obviate
this difficulty our concluding extract is written in the
glossic alphabet invented by Mr. Alexander J. Ellis,

F.R.S., for the representation of ordinary English and
its varied dialects.

KOARTI'N TOYM.

———

Uv oa· th)toymz u)th dai· un niyt,
  Thur)z won ut au· loyk th)baest;
It kuumz wi')th diyi'n u)th liyt,
  Waen th)suon uz gon tu raest.

Un waen th)uuwd tlok iz uopu)th st'roa·k,
  Mi' aart iz rae·r un fai·n;
Au donz mi' swing'ur on, un guoz
  Tu miyt mi' swiytaart Jai·n.

Un waen tu)th wuodn brij au kuum,
  Ut)s tloa·s bi' Laangli'·Liy;
Au staarts u wisli'n 'dhaen loyk maad,
  Til th)brid kuumz uuwt tu miy.

Un boy uuwd Pind'u'r mil wi' goo·,
  Un duuwn bi')th bruok soyd wau·k;
Un pae·rti'n toym uz au·lu'z kuum,
  Ufoa·r we')n duon uuwr tau·k.

Ai· ! th)fluuwu'rz i' ivu'ri' loa·n now noa·z,
  Thur nai·mz bi' aart uow)z got;
Un in mi' koou't laast niyt uow puot
  U bluow fu'rgyaet·mi'·not.

Un dhaat, bi')th maas, au nivu'r shaal,
  Uz luong uz au·)m u sinu'r;
Un iv uow iz bu'r tu bi' wuon,
  Bi')th maaski'nz dhaen au)l win u'r.

Translated into book English from " Dr. Rondeau's Revenge," and other Lancashire sketches.

COURTING TIME.

Of all the times of the day and night,
Ther's one that I like the best,
It comes with the dying of the light,
When the sun has gone to rest.

And when the old clock is upon the stroke,
My heart is rare and fain ;
I don my swinger on, and go
To see my sweetheart Jane.

And when to the wooden bridge I come,
That's close by Langley-lea,
I start a-whistling then like mad,
Till the bird comes owt to me.

And by old Pinder's mill we go,
And down by the brookside walk,
And parting time has always come,
Before we've done our talk.

Ah ! the flowers in ev'ry lane she knows,
Their names by heart she's got;
And in my coat, last night, she put
A blue Forget-Me-Not.

And that by the mass I never shall
As long as I'm a sinner,
And if she is but to be won,
By the maskins then I'll win her.

The following will show the precise value of the

glossic symbols employed in the above extract; for
further details we must refer to Mr. Ellis's lecture,
delivered before the Society of Arts, April 20th,
1870 :—

1. ee   beer=beeu'r.
2. i   *fit.*
3. ai   n*a*me=naim
4. ae   p*ai*r=pae'r.
          bed=báed.
          pet=pa'et.
5. aa   b*aa*.
          *a*rt=áart.
          f*a*t=faat.
6. au   c*a*ll=kau.
          I unemphatic au.
7. o   n*o*t.
8. uu   l*o*ve=luuv.
          t*u*rn=túurn.
9. oa   c*oa*l.
          d*o*main=doamain.
10. uo   c*u*p=kuop.
          s*o*n=súon.
11. oo   p*oo*r=poou'r (The Northern short *u*).
12. i'   pit*y*=piti'.
          com*i*ng=kuumi'ng.
13. u'   ment*io*n=maenshu'n.
          w*a*ter=waut'u'r.
2 & 1.   i*ee*=iy; *see*=siy; *feel*=fiyl.
10 & 11. u*ooo*=uow; cool=kuowl.
Long i=oy.
Long u—initial=yoo; humour=yoomu'r
          medial or final iw or eew; tune=ti'wn or teewn.

E

4 & 1.   aeee= aey ; weight=waeyt.
8 & 11.   uuoo=uuw; *out*=uuwt.
tl for cl ; clock=*tl*ok.
dl for gl ; gloppent=*dl*opnt.
dental t ; t' tree=t'riy ; water=wait'u'r.
dental d ; d' drink=d'rink.
     fodder=fod'd'u'r.
Palatal k=k' ; cart=kyaart.
Palatal g=g' ; garden=gyaardi'n.

The first column contains the glossic symbols or notation for the vowels, dipthongs, and peculiar consonantal sounds in the South Lancashire dialect; and the second column the key words in which the sounds of the glossic symbols are printed in *italics*.

ACCENT.—Place a stress on the first syllable when not otherwise marked.

QUANTITY OF VOWELS.—All vowels are to be read short or medial, except otherwise marked.

THE STRESS (ˑ) placed immediately after a vowel shows it to be long and accented, as *auˑgust*; placed immmediately after a consonant, it shows that the preceding vowel is short and accented, as *augusˑt*.

DIVIDER) , occasionally used to assist the reader by separating to the eye words not separated to the ear, as *tael)ur dhaet)l duow*.

Several of these sounds do not occur in conventional English. The most noticeable is (uuw) which has been not inappropriately called the Lancashire Shibboleth, and (aey) which, although not recognised by the dictionaries, appears still to linger in the words

eight, weight, freight, which are often marked to
rhyme with hate, fate, &c., although their general
pronunciation is very distinct from the vowel (ai) in
those words.

"The leading characteristics of the South Lancashire dialect," says Mr. Picton, "may be comprised
under the following heads :—1. Obsolete and peculiar
words and phraseology ; 2. Peculiar grammatical
forms ; 3. Peculiar contractions in the combination of
words; 4. Peculiarity of pronunciation."*

Mr. Thomas Heywood, the Rev. John Davies, the
Rev. Wm. Gaskell, Mr. Picton, and the late Mr. Harland
have, in the several memoirs on the subject, so well
examined the philological structure of the dialect
that nothing fresh remains to be said. The dialect
retains traces of all the various tribes by whom the
district has been peopled, the preponderating element
being Anglo-Saxon. Mr. Gaskell gives observations
on the etymology of 177 words or phrases. Of these
29 appear to be of Keltic origin, and the remainder
Teutonic, generally derived from the Anglo-Saxon,
although, in some cases, more probable roots may be
found in the other Gothic dialects. These represent
the influence of the old Frisian section of the early
settlers, and of the Danes, whose settlements have
given names to several places in the county. Mr.
Picton has examined 222 words, and assigns 54 of

* Trans. Literary and Philosophical Society of Liverpool,
xix., 24.

them to a Welsh origin, 15 to old Frisian, 100 to Anglo-Saxon, 40 to Danish, and 13 to Norman French.

There appears to be gaining ground a belief that the influence of the Kelts in the formation of the English race has been underrated. The theory of their almost total extinction by the Anglo-Saxons has long been received without much examination. In Lancashire, at all events, they have left their mark upon the language of the people. It has been said, however, that Lancashire is the most Keltic county in England.

The grammatical peculiarities of the dialect are generally owing to the retention of old forms of expression, which have either dropped out of conventional English or become corrupted. Thus *hoo* (she) is the Anglo-Saxon personal feminine pronoun, and *um* is not a construction of them as might at first be thought, but the Anglo-Saxon *heom*. *Axen, brast,* &c., are more ancient than ask and burst. The termination of verbs in *en*, which may be found in Chaucer and Pier's Ploughman, is retained in the dialect. The plural ending in *en* may be seen in *een, shoon, kine* (from cy' A.S.). It is to be regretted that the sibillant *s* has almost universally replaced this more euphonious form in the sign of the plural. "If," says Sir Francis Doyle, "we could call back from oblivion and disuse that valuable termination in *en*, it is impossible to say what metrical triumphs might not be achieved. We might even hope to allay, if we could not fully quench, the disembodied hiss which floats round a church, whenever the school children pause in their hymn."*

The tendency to contractions is very great, rendering some sentences unintelligible to a "foreigner." *Luthee preo* (look thee, pray you); *mitch goodeeto* (much good may it do you).

The peculiarities of our folk-speech will be best seen by the following miniature glossary, in which will be found an explanation of all the words that occur in the preceding extracts, and differ materially from conventional English. From the occasional notes appended, it will be seen that in many cases we have retained archaic forms in the dialect which have disappeared from the literary language.

Ax = ask (Acsian, axian A. S.) "Therefor nyle ze be made like to hem, for youre fadir woot what is nede to zou; before that ye axen him." Wiclif. Test. 1380. Matt. vi. 8. Axe is used in Tyndall's version of 1534, whilst Cranmer, five years later, employs aske.

Bawks = baulks.

Beawn = bound. "Now, in Icelandic buinn is the participle of bua, signifying prepared, addressed to, or, as we have the word somewhat disguised in English, 'bound for.' In old English, we have the word as 'boun'."—*Gaskell.*

Blash = a blaze, a flash, a sudden burst, as "a blash o' foyar" or "leetnin'." Blash-boggart may mean

* Lectures on Poetry, p. 58.

an apparition that appears for an instant, then disappears. *Blash* = (*blœce* A.S. paleness?)

Boggart = a spirit, an apparition, a ghost or goblin. "In welsh Bogelu signifies to affright. The root of the word, which is bwg, is not unlikely to be that from which boggart, or buggart, is derived." —*Gaskell.*

Brawsen = bursting, burst, bursted. Also glutted (Braisg, Welsh, coarse.)

Brids = birds. (Briddes, A.S.—"The young of any bird or animal."—*Bosworth.* "Briddis of heuene han nestis."—Wiclif's Test. 1380. Also, metaphorically, children, as, "Ther's o bonny show o' brids i'th' nest."

Clinkert = sound of metals. (Klincken, Dutch.) Clink, clinker, from clinch = a smart blow, a ringing slap, a "run bar punse;" clinker=a jingling sound; also a strong, large-headed nail used for heavy country shoes ; also a large crossled cinder or salamander; clinker't—crossled ; also the noise made when a person walks over flags with clinkered shoes on.

Cratch=(Créche, French.) a rack for hay in a stable.

Crinkum-crankums==odds and ends, curiosities.

Dithert=trembled, quaked.

Doff=do off, take off.

Een=eyes. (Eágan A.S.)

Eigh=aye, yes ; also an interjection meaning, "Is it so?" Eigh-eigh !=a strong affirmation. Eigh-lats! =a word to hie, encourage, or set on a dog. Eigh-lads-Eigh !=a phrase enjoining every one to haste and look out for himself.

Fare, fair, feor=Fær, A.S.—intense, great, actually, extreme. As "Fair frectont (or feeort);" "Fair cheeotin, &c." Fairation=fair play. Fair-faw (or fo')=fair fall *i. e.* good attend you; to happen well to; also preferable, as "Fair faw snow to rain." Fair-grand=splendid,

Fause, fawse=quick, intelligent, subtle, cunning, crafty. Also false, as the "fawsebothom" of a box; Fawse-loft = an attic or place of concealment.

Frimbles = tries ineffectually; shapes awkwardly as if "He're o' fingers un' thumbs."

Fuddle (? from foot-ale, beverage required from one entering a new occupation) = to tipple; a drinking bout; Fuddlt = fuddled, drunk; to make drunk, to intoxicate.

Gawm=to understand, to comprehend; to gather the meaning. Gyman A.S. attention. Heywood says gaumjau (Goth.) and geomian A.S., but this is doubtful; geomian—gieman is *to regard*, not *to understand*. The root appears to be Gothic as Mr. Gaskell points out, in which tongue Gaumidedun is they saw, they perceived.

Glendart=stared. Collier says A.S., which is doubtful. There is Glendrian A.S.—To swallow, devour, to gluttonize.—*Bosworth.*

Glooart=looked intently. Glære A.S. glare. Why *glore* thyn eyes in thy head? *Palsgrave*, 1540, quoted by Halliwell. It is given by Levins (1570).

Gloppen=to frighten; (Glop, Glupna, *Norse*, means to despond, to lose courage.) "Thowe wenys to

glopyne me with thy gret wordez." *Morte Arthure.*
(Halliwell.) Glop=to stare, to be surprised; Glop-
pen=to astonish, to stupify; Gloppen, gloppent=
surprised, amazed, frightened.

Gooah = go. Gá, A.S.=go.

Guts = " The guts are with us what the brains are to
other people. Butler seated the affections in this
part of the body : ' It grieved him to the guts that
they'—*Hudibras, part* 1, *canto* 2, *line* 893. ' *He has
no guts in his brains.*' ' The anfractus of the brain
looked upon when the dura mater is taken off, do
much resemble guts."—*Ray.* Heywood on Lanc.
Dial., p. 24.

Hadloontrean = the gutter or space between the head-
lands (or buts) and others. A.S. Rein, ren = rain ;
Renian=to rain. Ren, rin, rine, ryne=a gutter, a
water furrow, a watercourse.

Hal=a fool.

Hammil-scoance=Village Lantern ; satirically means
the hamlet (or village) Solomon. Sconce occurs
in Levins 1570, and in Minsheu.

Hoo=she. From heó, the third person feminine of
the A.S. personal pronoun.

Kersun=christen. (Kersten. Dutch.)

Kippo, kibbo=a long stick.

Kokink=a cocking-match. (Kok, coc, A.S.)

Kratchin=fad, whim, scheme or conceit.

Lawm=lame. (Lam, A.S.)

Lemme=let me

Limber=supple, flexible. This occurs in Minsheu.

Loppen=past tense of leap; also cropped.

Lukko=look you.

Lumber=mischief; damage; rubbish, *i. e.* old or odd valueless things.

Lunchin=luncheon.

Marlock=lark, frolic, vagary, antic, ridiculous gesture. Marlockin'—gambolling, playing.

Marrow=like, companion; a mate, an equal, a match.

> Busk ye, busk ye, my bonnie bride,
> Busk ye, my winsome *marrow*.
>
> Braes of Yarrow.

Maskins=a diminutive of "By the mass."

Meeterley=moderately, tolerably. Hollinshed uses this word (mœtre A.S.) Levins has *meetely*.

Mey=make.

Naygur=negro, used as an equivalent for hard, drudging labour.

Nomony, nominy=a wordy speech, recitation, or address; a profuse, formal address or invocation. Nomminies=long statements generally got by heart.

Owd=old. (Oud, Dutch.)

Pick'd=vomited; cast out; thrown, pitched; also woven, or thrown the weft once across the warp.

Pingot=a small croft near a house.

Plek=place (plæce A.S., a street, an open place) a spot.

Poo'd=pulled.

Potates=potatoes. This is generally pronounced as a word of two syllables, the termination being disused.

Powse-durt (Poussière, French, dust)=lumber, offal,

rubbish; a term of reproach. Mr. Gaskell suggests that this is from "the Welsh Pws, which means what is expelled or rejected, refuse."

Prompted. (Then Grace hoo prompted her featly and foine.) This means she made herself quite prim.

Reawk=(if fro that greawnd tha'll reawk. Bamford.) Bamford inserted this word to meet the exigencies of the rhyme. Reawk=to meet in neighbours houses and spend time in idle gossip. Reawkin'= sitting close; tarrying out at nights; meeting together. Reawk't=raked out at night; rooked; collected. Reawken—they rake, &c.; Reawken't =they raked, &c.

Rig=sport; a trick or frolic; also to jest.

Scoance=see Hammil Scoance.

Scratt=scratching. This occurs in Levins and is not an uncommon form in Early English. Black Scrat and Owd Scrat=the Devil.

Seawse=blow with the open hand, or hand partially open; a box or "clout" on the head; also to plunge or immerse. "And geve them a *sowce* with his hande." *Robert the Devyll* (quoted by Halliwell). Pig-seawse=potted pigs head.

Shoon=shoes. (Scón, sceón, A.S.)

Shutterin=slipping, sliding. An elongation of the A. S. Scítan, sceótan—to shoot.

Sidles=(sidles i' th' lone)—follows a lass bashfully and secretly.

Smudge=small or slack coals, as "smithy smudge." Also a stink or stench, as of smoky steam, when a smith puts water on his fire; also a hearty kiss; also to smear.

Snever=slender, smooth.

Snig=eel. (A.S. Snícan=to sneak, to creep?)

Snood=a fillet, cap, hood; artificial hair; a fillet to tie up a woman's hair. Snod A.S.

Sompan=a corruption of sample or example.

Sowght=sighed.

Spers=asks. (Spyrian A.S.—to ask. Speriend A.S. =an enquirer.)

Spon new=brand new.

Swaps=exchanges.

Swat=struck, so as to draw blood. (Swát A.S.)

Swoipt=drank at one breath or *swoop.*

Thrumper'd=thumped, beat with the clinched fist.

Tickle=particular, as a squeamish man; easily moved, as a trap when set; uncertain, as applied to the weather; excitable as to tickle a man's fancy.

Tone,=one, t'one or to'ther the one, or the other. "Tone, tother, oather'll do," is a not uncommon phrase.

Tougher=portion or dowry.

Udgit=idiot.

Um, em=them, (heom A.S. dative plural pronoun.) "Hem seemed hem han getten hem protection."

Chaucer.

Un, an=and. (Un, Dutch.)

Urchon=hedgehog.

Waistrel, (from waste)=a good-for-nothing article or

person; a scoundrel; primarily, an article spoiled during its fabrication.

Wammo=weakly; hungry and tired.

Warch=ache, pain. (Wærc, weorc, A.S.)

Wawtit=overturned, (Wæltan, wealtian, A.S.—to roll, reel, or stagger, to tumble.)

Welly=well nigh, almost.

Whack=a box or bump; a smart, loud blow; also, to thrash or beat; also alcoholic drink, as "He likes his whack;" also to share with, as "Theau'st whack wi' me."

Whackerin=trembling, quaking.

Whick=quick, alive.

Whoavt=turned.

Whoam=home. (Is not this the terribly aspirated A.S. Hám?)

Wisket=a large flat basket, without handle, and made of unpeeled twigs or osiers.

Woode=mad; stark-woode=stark mad. (Wód, A.S.)

Wough=weft.

Wur=was; were; also worse.

Yearnstful=earnestly, i. e., full of earnest.

Yo=you. (A.S. eow.)

Yure=hair. (Hær, A.S.)

When the Professor of Poetry in the University of Oxford devotes one of his lectures to the subject of "Provincial Poetry," and elucidates his remarks by quotations from poems written in the homely folk-speech of Dorsetshire, we may congratulate ourselves that the irrational prejudice against dialects is fast dying out, and is being succeeded by a more catholic spirit of criticism.

Philology has shown us their value, and many a curious relic of old world belief has been found fossilized in the provincial speech. Mr. W. Aldis Wright has suggested the compilation of a general Provincial glossary, and the formation of a society for its execution. It is to be hoped that the proposal will receive cordial support and be prosecuted to a successful issue. I venture here to reproduce a suggestion contributed to "Notes and Queries" of June 11th.

" Whilst fully agreeing with Mr. Wright as to the importance of the proposed work (and its desirability is so self-evident that it would be a waste of valuable space to insist upon it further), I would suggest that, instead of creating a new society to perform this special work, it should be done by the co-operation of societies already existing. The main difficulty about the compilation of the glossary would be the creation of an adequate machinery for the collection of words, and equally so for the arrangement of the rude material collected. The first would necessitate the presence of a committee of workers in every shire of the land. Might not the existing learned and literary societies furnish a machinery ready made for both these objects? The Royal Society, although founded for the "advancement of natural knowledge," pays so little attention to anything but natural philosophy, that its co-operation could perhaps not be counted upon, in spite of Dr. Max Müller's vindication of philology as one of the physical sciences. But the Society of Antiquaries, the Royal Society of Literature, the Ethnological Society, the Philological Society, and the Anthropological Society in England; the Royal Society of Edinburgh, the Society of Antiquaries of Scotland in North Britain; and the Royal Hibernian Academy in Ireland, could certainly furnish a better staff of collectors than would be otherwise obtained. There should be added to this list also the local literary societies (some of which, the Literary and Philosophical Society of Liverpool and the Historic Society of Lancashire and Cheshire for instance, have published in their Transactions valuable papers relating to dialects), and also printing clubs of the character of the Camden, Chetham, and Surtees, the Early English Text, Chaucer and Ballad Societies.

"A provincial glossary would be so great a gain to archæology, ethnology, and philology, and would throw such new light upon the English language, manners, and customs, that the associations devoted to those branches of knowledge could not fail to be interested in the success of the undertaking. A circular addressed to them would, I feel certain, bring forth a cordial response. Their members might constitute in each district a local committee, "with power to add workers to their number;" and this enlargement might proceed until all the students of folk-speech were included in the network. A point of great importance is that the collectors of words should record them uniformly—in fact, is the old difficulty about the absurdly unphonetic nature of our ordinary orthography and its entire unfitness for representing dialectic shades of pronunciation. The alphabet of Mr. Isaac Pitman, although well fitted for representing the sounds of conventional English, is also inadequate for the purpose. A few years ago this would have been a serious difficulty, but the physiological alphabet (so long despaired of) has at last been invented. In Melville Bell's *Visible Speech* we have a scientific and exact registering of all spoken sounds, and in the glossotype (and glossic) of Mr. Ellis, we have the scheme adapted to our ordinary type.

"The forthcoming volume of Mr. Ellis's *Early English Pronunciation* containing the section on English dialects will, no doubt, contain valuable material for the proposed glossary. The aid of the accomplished author of this important work will be of the greatest service. There are other portions of the subject which require careful consideration, but a regard for the patience of both editor and reader leads me to postpone any remarks upon them, and to content myself with urging the advisability of compiling, concurrently with the glossary, a bibliography of the literature of provincial dialects. Some of the dialects are very rich in tales and poems. Perhaps the most extensively cultivated is that of South Lancashire. A bibliography of works in this dialect, which is now being prepared for the press, contains about two hundred titles." *

* The bibliography here alluded to has since been published

There have been several essays at a Lancashire glossary. Collier has appended one to his "Tummus and Meary," in which he has occasionally marked the Anglo-Saxon derivations. Mr. Bamford's amended edition of "Tim Bobbin" includes an enlarged glossary. Finally, Mr. John Higson, whose wide acquaintance with the dialect and its literature make him peculiarly eligible for the task, is now preparing one which will be of great value, as it is the fruit of years of patient observation and study.

Though the greater part of the Lancashire lyrics are written in the folk speech, our poetical treasures are by no means limited to that class of composition. True, there are few romantic or legendary ballads; for Lancashire, although rich in traditions of the past, is singularly deficient in those rhyming records of them, which appear to be so common in some counties. Bamford's " Wild Rider," the "Billmen of Bowland," and Ainsworth's capital ballad of " Old Grindrod's Ghost," are enough to redeem the county from the charge of poverty.

In "love songs and praises of the fair" we have a long array of lyrics, from which we may learn how Dan Cupid rules hearts among our Lancashire cloughs and gloomy streets. What can be more beautiful than this portrait of

under the title of " The Literature of the Lancashire Dialect," a bibliographical essay, London : Trübner & Co., and records the titles (with occasional annotations) of two hundred and seventy-nine publications illustrative of this dialect.

MARGARET.

—

Artist's chisel could not trace
Such a form, with so much grace ;
Never in Italian skies
Dwells such light as in her eyes.
Sweeter music ne'er was sung
Than hangs ever on her tongue.
Roses have not such a glow
As that upon her brilliant brow ;
All that's bright and fair are met
In lovely, charming Margaret.

This is from a poem which was written by William Rowlinson, a canvasser for a local directory, who was drowned whilst bathing in the Thames.

The love songs of Swain and Rogerson are well known, as also Mr. Bealey's lovely " Sweetheart Maggie." Not so well known, however, is Mr. Thos. A. Tidmarsh's poem of " Cupid's Love Draught "—one of the richest and sweetest love songs in the language. We quote a verse :—

" I will gather the smiles of the fairest of women,"
    Said Cupid one evening to me,
" In a goblet of wine for thy spirit to swim in,
    And bring it all glowing to thee,
      If thou'lt swear by the cup,
      Ere thou drainest it up,
That thou'lt worship no maiden beside,
      And affirm by the shine
      Of her smiles in the wine
That thou'lt woo her and make her thy bride ;

F

> And she shall be lustre and glory to thee,
> Enchanting thy bosom with heaven-born glee;
> For she is the brightest and loveliest thing
> That ever I pressed with the down of my wing."

Then follows a gorgeous vision of fair women, dowered with "beauty and splendour," with "hearts young and tender, which felt not, which dreamt not of care," but among the glittering throng he looks in vain for the promised maiden, but as he is about to depart, she sits down by his side,

> Round a goblet her tapering white fingers did twine
> Like lilies, and blushing she bent
> O'er the brim to behold her dark eyes in the wine,
> Which retained all the lustre they'd lent.

If the Lancashire lad is an impassioned wooer, he is equally faithful as a husband, and kind as a father, the home-affections twine close round his heart, and he loves to celebrate the joys of the fireside,

> Where the calm tender tones of affection are heard;
> Where the child's gladsome carol is ringing;
> Where the heart's best emotions are quicken'd and stirr'd
> By the founts that are inwardly springing.

As examples we may refer to Mr. Proctor's "Early Haunts revisited," J. C. Prince's "As Welcome as Flowers in May," Samuel Bamford's lines addressed to his wife during her recovery from a long illness,—

> Full thirty years have o'er us pass'd
> Since thou and I were wed,
> And time hath dealt us many a blast,
> And somewhat bowed thy head,

And torn thin thy bright brown hair,
That stream'd so wild and free,
But oh ! thy tresses still art fair,
And beautiful to me !

Another home lyric of the same class is

THE KISS BENEATH THE HOLLY.

By Mrs. Hobson Farrand.

"Be merry and wise," says the good old song,
And joy to the heart that penn'd it;
If we've ought to fret, the stately "pet"
Will never reform or mend it.
On Christmas night, when the log burns bright,
To be joyous is not folly;
There's nought amiss in the playful kiss
That's stolen beneath the holly.

Let hand clasp hand with a hearty clasp,
To all give a welcome greeting;
Fling pride afar; don't gloom or mar
The coming Christmas meeting.
"Be merry and wise," say sparkling eyes,
Away with all melancholy—
There's nought amiss, just laugh at the kiss
That's stolen beneath the holly.

Oh, welcome with glee the festive night,
When the joyous bells are ringing;
But once a year the chime we hear,
That the Christmas time is bringing.
Don't pout or frown 'neath the mystic crown—
To be joyous is not folly;
There's nought amiss in the Christmas kiss
That's stolen beneath the holly.

It would be unjust to pass on without mentioning one writer of whom Lancashire will one day be proud. Mr. Dawson's lyrics are noticeable for their careful finish, subtle thoughtfulness, and tender, sombre gracefulness. Take for example

TWILIGHT.

Day is dying, ploughed with scars ;
　Night takes up the reins of time,
Driving careful, till the stars—
Lamps, to light her countless cars—
Gleam athwart yon amber bars,
　Royal, radiant, and sublime.

And through space that has no bound,
　Grim old Silence—older far
Than his sprightlier brother, Sound—
Heaves and palpitates around,
Breathless, faint, as Age is found
　Ever where the Seasons are.

And the zephyrs have no rest,
　To embrace the willing corn,
And the stilly skies no quest
'Till the quiet of the west
Makes a motion of its rest
　As the evening winds are born.

Fainter fades the dim daylight,
　Falling like some sweet song sent
Wandering on the winds at night,
Wavering till it dies outright,
Slow dissolved, as if by blight,
　To its native element.

Songs of life and brotherhood are numerous, preaching for the most part a gospel of cheerfulness, labour, and contentment. Of this nature is Mr. Charles Swain's poem,

BE KIND TO EACH OTHER.

Be kind to each other!
  The night's coming on,
When friend and when brother
  Perchance may be gone!
Then midst our dejection,
  How sweet to have earn'd
The blest recollection
  Of kindness—return'd.
When day hath departed
  And memory keeps
Her watch—broken hearted—
  Where all she loved sleeps.

Let falsehood assail not—
  Nor envy disprove,—
Let trifles prevail not,
  Against those ye love.
Nor change with the morrow
  Should fortune take wing,
But the deeper the sorrow
  The closer still cling!

Some of Bamford's finest writings belong to this class, "The Song for the Brave," and the gloomy "Pass of Death."

In devotional poetry, we have already named the grand carol—"Christians Awake"—but it would be unjust to close our imperfect review without noticing the sacred poetry of Mrs. T. D. Crewdson.

In her case, Faith and Imagination have kissed together; Religion and Poesy have embraced. We offer in justification, this—

THANKSGIVING FOR THE HARVEST.

For the sunshine and the rain,
  For the dew and for the shower,
For the yellow, ripened grain,
  And the golden harvest hour,
    We bless Thee, oh our God!

For the heat and for the shade,
  For the gladness and the grief,
For the tender sprouting blade,
  And for the nodding sheaf,
    We bless Thee, oh our God!

For the hope and for the fear,
  For the storms and for the peace,
For the trembling and the cheer,
  And for the glad increase,
    We bless Thee, oh our God!

Our hands have tilled the sod,
  And the torpid seed have sown;
But the quickening was of God,
  And the praise be His alone.
    We bless Thee, oh our God!

For the sunshine and the shower,
  For the dew and for the rain,
For the golden harvest hour,
  And for the garnered grain,
    We bless Thee, oh our God!

There are certain characteristics which are more or less shared by all these productions, and which somewhat puzzle us for a definition of poetry which shall fairly include all these outpourings of the Lancashire singer. He is no grand minstrel, setting forth, in words sublime, the bloody triumphs of the battle-fields, nor does he indite a "woeful baliad to his mistress' eyebrows;" his songs are not of blossoming hawthorn and the golden sun of June, nor of the war and strife of human passions in their highest intensity ; and yet his strains are truest poetry, and instinct with human interest.

The short and simple annals of the poor, their virtues, loves, and failings,—these are the subjects of his rhymes, and fitter subjects for poets of this class could not be found than the working men of Lancashire. The genuine Lancashire lad is a being worthy of study ; his deep sense of humour, his patient endurance of adversity, his life-long struggle with want, his indomitable perseverance, his love of home—all point him out as one of a remarkable race ; and, despite his sometimes rough exterior and uncouth language, your real Lancashire lad is one of nature's gentlemen at heart.

And well have these characteristics been reproduced by men like Edwin Waugh, Benjamin Brierley, Sam. Bamford, Samuel Laycock, and others. These men have been, to a great extent, self-educated, themselves a portion of the people whom they describe ; and their pictures may therefore be taken, not as the random expressions of a casual stranger, but as the conclusions of persons thoroughly acquainted with the men whose lives and feelings they describe with such humour, pathos, and dramatic power, and running through their writings is a vein of tenderest humanity, of brotherly love for their fellow men, however degraded by sin and misery.

L. of C.

DURING the present age the rapid diffusion of knowledge has happily driven forth much antique superstition; but there is a temptation to exaggerate the extent of the effects which have thus been produced, and few people, we fancy, would credit the ignorance and credulity that yet exist in civilized England.

It is not impossible, gentle reader, that in your own vicinity there are persons who practise with a thorough conviction of their efficacy, charms which may once have formed part of the Druidic, or some still older religious ceremonial: people who consult the "Golden Dream Book" every morning, who have faith in "cunning women" and "wise men," who would'nt walk under a ladder on any account, who shudder if salt is spilled at the table, and who cry "God bless you" to one who sneezes, just as they did in Rome two thousand years ago.

A little inquiry will show that the lower orders especially are particularly conservative of their unwritten belief, for the most part one of great antiquity, and including articles which once formed integral portions of mythologic systems long since superseded by a purer faith. "Indeed," say our authors, "Folk-lore superstitions may be said to be the debris of ancient mythologies, it may be of India or Egypt, Greece or Rome, Germany or Scandinavia.

Some of the opinions and observances which are called by the general name of folk-lore, are perfectly innocent in themselves, and have so quaint an air that one hardly desires to see them abolished, but the majority are objectionable in every respect, and the sooner they become extinct the better.

In Lancashire, where we might have expected to find that the noise of the steam-engine had frightened away both the fairies and the queen of the May, and the spread of knowledge to have destroyed all faith in spells and charms, Messrs. Harland and Wilkinson have collected sufficient of this floating traditionary folk-lore to make a goodly and interesting volume. Many years attention to this subject has enabled them to produce a book which contains a careful summary of Lancashire superstition, and which is of considerable value to the student of anthropology and mythology.* The collection is a very complete one, though no doubt the interest attendant upon the publication of this work, will bring to light many more curious fragments of old wife's learning.

Many observances are connected with particular seasons of the year. Thus on New Year's day there is a firm belief that if a light-haired person "let in" the New Year, a twelve month of ill-luck will be the re-

* Lancashire Folk Lore, compiled and edited by John Harland, F.S.A., and T. T. Wilkinson, F.R.A.S. London: F. Warne, 1867.

sult, and that on the contrary dark persons will bring with them a year of good fortune.

So Pan-cake Tuesday, Simnel Sunday, Easter, May Day, Christmas, etc., have each their special customs still observed in Lancashire, though in many cases so shorn of their ancient glories as to be little more than relics of former greatness.

The habit of attaching a symbolic importance even to the most trifling occurrences, is strikingly illustrated in the following quotations :

"Most grandmothers will exclaim, ' God bless you!' when they hear a child sneeze, and they sum up the philosophy of the subject with the following lines, which used to delight the writer in the days of his childhood :

' Sneeze on a Monday, you sneeze for danger ;
Sneeze on a Tuesday, you kiss a stranger ;
Sneeze on a Wednesday, you sneeze for a letter ;
Sneeze on a Thursday, for something better ;
Sneeze on a Friday, you sneeze for sorrow ;
Sneeze on a Saturday, your sweetheart to-morrow,
Sneeze on a Sunday, your safety seek,
The Devil will have you the whole of the week."

This is certainly a comprehensive epitome of the entire philosophy of sneezing. Equally precise are the lines relating to the cutting of the finger nails :

"Cut your nails on a Monday, cut them for news ;
Cut them on Tuesday, a pair of new shoes,"

In connection with this part of the subject, we once chanced to hear a bit of Lancashire folk-lore which we have not noticed in the present volume, that is, that the finger nails of a baby should be *bit* shorter.

If they are cut, the child will become "sharp fingered"
—*i.e.*, thievish.

The inhabitants of Cockerham, having made up
their minds that the devil had been showing an un-
reasonable partiality to their village, gave the schoolmaster the not very pleasant task of expelling the
Prince of Darkness from their midst. The man of
letters having raised the foul fiend appointed him
three tasks; if he failed to accomplish them he was
never to appear again at Cockerham, but if he succeeded in their performance, the pedagogue became his prey.
The two first tasks were soon done, but the third, the
fatal, mystic third—

"Now make me, dear sir, a rope of yon sand,
Which will bear washing in Cocker, and not lose a strand"—

proved too much even for the ingenuity of the Father
of Evil, and if he stuck to his bargain Cockerham
must be the happiest place on earth! This legend of
the Three Tasks, we may remark, is not confined to
Lancashire, but is also narrated in connection with
Merton Sands, Cheshire, and a Cornish version forms
the subject of one of the Rev. R. S. Hawker's wildest
lyrics.

"The parochial church at Burnley," it is said, "was
originally intended to be built on the site occupied by
the old Saxon Cross in Godly Lane; but however much
the masons might have built during the day, both
stones and scaffolding were invariably found where
the church now stands, on their coming to work next
morning." "This legend," say the editors, "is told

also of Rochdale, Winwick, and Samlesbury churches," to which we may add that it is also attached to the churches of Over, Saddleworth, and Churchdown, and many others.

A winding sheet in the candle, spilling the salt, crossing knives, and various other trifles, are omens of evil to thousands at this day. Should one of your children fall sick when on a visit at a friend's house, it is held to be sure to entail bad luck on that family for the rest of the year, if you stay over New Year's Day Persons have been known to travel sixty miles with a sick child, rather than run the risk. A flake of soot on the bars of the grate, is said to indicate the approach of a stranger; a bright spark on the wick of a candle, or a long piece of stalk in the tea-cup, betokens a similar event. When the fire burns briskly, some lover smirks or is good-humoured. A cinder thrown out of the fire by a jet of gas from burning coals, is looked upon as a coffin if its hollow be long; as a purse of gold if the cavity be roundish. Crickets in houses are said to indicate good fortune; but should they forsake the chimney corner, it is a sure sign of coming misfortune.

We learn that in the Fylde the following charm is still used for the cure of tooth-ache :—

> " Peter sat weeping on a marble stone,
> Jesus came near and said, ' What aileth thee, O Peter ?'
> He answered and said, ' My Lord and my God !'
> He that can say this, and believe it for my sake,
> Never more shall have the toothache."

Our " wise men " still sell the following charm for
the cure of continued toothache, but it must be worn
inside the vest or stays, and over the left breast:—

"As Sant Petter sat at the geats of Jerusalm our blessed
Lord and Sevour Jesus Crist pased by and sead, ' What eleth
thee,' he sead, ' Lord my teeth ecketh,' he sead, ' Arise and follow me, and thy teeth shall never eake eney moor. Fiat †
Fiat † Fiat †

From the wide range of the subject it is impossible
to take all its branches into consideration here; but
sufficient has, perhaps, been done to show the interesting character of the book If we could look upon its contents entirely as relics of the past, the pleasure would be greater; but nonsense of this sort is
still firmly believed in by many; a fact that should
give a slight shock to that spirit of complacency with
which we are apt to glorify the " wondrous, wondrous
age." We do not look at this mass of ignorance
honestly and frankly, but try to deceive ourselves
that it does not exist, and so leave it to fester and
corrupt the very life-blood of the community.

" Superstition," says Theophrastus, "proceeds from
unworthy conceptions of the Deity." As the people
become mentally and spiritually enlightened, these
relics of heathendom will disappear from the national
mind ; the shades of darkness will roll away, and
vanish from the sky as the bright sun arises in his
power and might, heralding another and a brighter
day.

INDEX.

INDEX.

Tubbs & Brook, Printers, 11, Market Street, Manchester.